The Other Side

Stories

by

Cheney Duesler

The Other Side

Copyright © 2008 by Cheney Duesler. All rights reserved.
Published in the United States of America by Fireweed Press, Madison, Wisconsin. Printed by Inkwell Printers, Dodgeville, Wisconsin; pre-press work by Deena Vinger and Mitch Marty.

This is a work of fiction. Names, characters, places and incidents are either the product of the author's imagination or are used fictitiously. Any resemblance to actual persons, living or dead, events, or locales is coincidental.

Some of these stories appeared previously in the following:
Above the Bridge; *Fiction International*; *Keltic Fringe*; *Madison Magazine*; *Mediphors*; *Midwest Radio Theatre Workshop Annual Scriptbook 1998*; *Nimrod International Journal of Poetry & Prose*; *Passager*; *Radio Drama Awards 1977*; *The Writers Place Contest Anthology 1994*. Some of the stories were presented in readings at Brave Hearts Theatre, Madison, Wisconsin.

A version of this collection was a finalist in the 1994 Minnesota Voices Project competition.

With special thanks to Jeri McCormick, who edited this collection with the assistance of Robin Chapman. Thanks also to Dr. Harold Hurwitz, Berlin, Germany, and to the members of my manuscript group for their critiques and encouragement:

Bert Adams	Arthur Madson
Margaret Benbow	Jeri McCormick
Robin Chapman	Richard Roe
Lenore Coberly	Lynn Patrick Smith
Alice D' Alessio	Jim Stevens
CX Dillhunt	Betsy Strand
Nancy Jacobsen	Karen Updike

Cover photograph by Paul W. Duesler: Lake Michigan shore rocks near Fayette, Michigan
Cover design by Amy Kittleson

ISBN 1-878660-21-7

For Lenore McComas Coberly

who invited me to join her manuscript group
in 1987 and changed my life

The Other Side

Stories by
Cheney Duesler

Dyckman Street	9
We Have Birds	17
The Poetry Evening	21
Dining with Anita and Morris	27
Jari	39
Mr. Karas	53
Perceptions	61
Seija	65
The Revolutionary	73
Lake Superior Journal	77
Settling In	85
Kata	91
Getting On With It	99
Helmut	109
Post-Mortem	117
Shard	127
A Question of Performance	131
The Other Side	139
Visiting Mother This Summer	145
Plastics	149

Dyckman Street

NICK ROSS glances around his room, trying to see it through the eyes of his visiting nurse. He's stashed the liquor, emptied ash trays, and is in the process of picking up when someone knocks.

Instead of his nurse, Willie opens the door. "Hey mah man," Willie calls, "you pick a winner?"

"I could use it," Nick says.

Willie takes the dollar from the green bowl, copies the numbers, writes a receipt, and drops the stub in the bowl. "Nice day," Willie says. "Really warming up."

"Make me a winner," Nick calls after him. So, it's finally warming up. Might mean a visit from Pearl. She's so fragile lately, he's hardly seen her all winter. He glances at the clock. His nurse is running late and Willie's early. Their paths have converged a couple of times, but Willie's cool. One glance at her uniform and Willie says, "Just lookin' in, ma'am. Anything you need?" "What a nice person," Miss Grossman said.

Nick throws an empty cigarette carton and a few articles of clothing into the curtained alcove that contains his bed. He's spreading newspaper on the table when she knocks.

Miss Grossman thrusts her head in first as though uncertain the rest of her is welcome. "Nick," she exults, pleased he's remembered the newspapers.

She folds her uniform coat over a wooden chair. One deep breath indicates she's ready for him as she sits, straight-backed, watching him with clear blue eyes. "Well," she says, "how's it going?"

Nick knows she's running late. He can skip details. "I really feel better," he says. "I was just telling Manny yesterday that I think I'm stronger."

She's elated. "You see, your diet's paying off."

Last month she had reviewed his diet, registered horror, and outlined a nourishing inexpensive regime that made him sick just thinking about it. He had, however, had Manny pick up cereal and powdered milk and for several visits made a point of leaving the open boxes on the table just to make her eyes glisten.

"Now to business," she says, sitting before him and grasping his wrist and elbow to begin the first movements of his range of motion. Nick closes his eyes. He finds the beginning manipulations enjoyable. Her explanations never vary and her delicate, officious little probings send tingles up the back of his neck. The motions become progressively expansive until they border on the point of pain. He pretends real pain, saying bravely, "Go ahead, I know it won't get better without pain." He can never resist looking at her at this point. Brows furrowed, eyes intent on his twisted face, she all but collapses when he cries out. It's the best part of the visit.

"Is my range any better?" he asks when the exercises are completed. He can see she doesn't want to lie. "It takes time," she says, a line of concern twitching one eye. "Is Manny still conscientious? Does he exercise your arm every day?"

"Faithful as a spaniel," Nick says, wondering if Manny would remember any of the instructions she gave six months ago. He watches her wash her hands and get into her coat, knowing she will say something encouraging before she leaves. "It's getting warm, almost like spring," she says. "It won't be long before you're down on the front stoop, taking in the sun."

He hangs his head. "Yeah." He loves manipulating her into these last statements.

"Remember," she says, coming forward, squatting before him to capture his eyes with her mother look. "Remember that the arm and hand are always last to come back after a stroke."

"Yeah," he says still looking down.

"Just see how quickly your leg came back and you've never had any speech problems."

He looks up and gives her a wan, brave smile. He can see she's moved. She pats his hand. "I'll see you next week, Nick."

Nick falls asleep during the Game Show and the next thing he knows Pearl is bending over him. She looks terrible; make-up streaked, mascara making hollows of her eyes.

"Brandy Wine's dead," she says, beginning to wail, covering her mouth with both hands.

Nick's never heard such a sound. "What happened?"

"She was fifteen years old," Pearl chokes. "That's old for a dog, but she was so healthy; never sick." He watches her bony shoulders hunch and shake with grief.

"Aw Pearl, I'm sorry. When did it happen?"

"Sunday. I would a come over right away, but it was sleeting." She turns to him, "I know you loved her too. You're the only one who didn't call her a little rat or something terrible, the only one who understands." Again Pearl is racked by sobs. Nick wonders what gives her the idea he liked Brandy Wine. More than once he'd felt like murdering the animal who relieved herself wherever she pleased.

"I took her everywhere," Pearl says. "I'd just tuck her under my coat, and we could go to the movies, even McDonald's."

Nick nods. He knows this. "What did you do with her body?" he asks.

Pearl perks up. "That's what I want to talk about."

"Why don't you first get us a drink?" Nick says. Pearl puts the glasses on the table, lights two cigarettes and puts one in his mouth. "I've got her outside on my kitchen window sill," she says.

"On your window sill?" He can see she's trying to control herself enough to talk.

"What am I supposed to do, put her in the garbage? Put Brandy Wine in a dumpster?" Pearl's eyes bulge at him as she smashes her cigarette. "I can't part with her little body. Oh Nick, she looks so sweet, like she's sleeping out there."

"Yeah Pearl, that's fine in the winter, but it's warming up."

"That's what I want to talk to you about," she says, blotting her eyes. "You know how your super is always planting trees and things on the roof? I was thinking we could put Brandy Wine in one of them huge pots and then Nick, Nick, I could come over and sit with her. I don't want her being lonely." Pearl's off again. "I'm so sick of crying," she says, taking in a deep breath. "I'd feel good knowing where she is. I checked on that animal graveyard up in the Heights and besides being just for the rich, I would have to take two transfers just to get there. Nick you told me yourself that the super said you could go up on the roof any time. He'd give you a key."

At this point Nick will promise anything. "Manny can help us," he says.

Pearl throws her arms around him, backs off to blow her nose. "I have to get home, I just can't leave her for long."

That evening, before Bob and Lewis arrive for cards, Nick tells Manny Pearl's dog has died.

"That little rat? I wouldn't call that no dog," Manny says, refilling Nick's glass without taking his eyes off TV.

"Yeah, well it's like a kid to Pearl and she wants us to bury it, on the roof, in one of the Super's pots."

Manny laughs. "Can you imagine the stink?"

"I don't think so if we cover it real good," Nick says.

Manny lifts his undershirt and scratches his stomach. "You could make it easy on us by dumping the dog down the dumbwaiter and telling Pearl which pot's got her pooch. It's not like she's going to dig it up."

Nick shrugs. "Yeah, but I wouldn't feel right." He can feel Manny looking a hole through him. "What the hell's keeping Bob and Lewis?" he says. "Are we going to play cards or what?"

Nick's nurse is excited when she visits the following week. She asks the usual things, but Nick can tell her mind's somewhere else. "You got a secret," he says. "You going to get married or something?"

She laughs, sits at the table, her eyes shining. "Nick, I couldn't tell you until it was certain, but three months ago I put your name on a list for summer camp."

"Summer camp?"

"Not really a camp, but a lodge for people with handicaps. It's in the Adirondacks, has its own swimming pool, a lake out front, let me show you." She pulls a brochure from her coat showing the marvels of the place. "It's for two weeks, all expenses paid." Nick's flabbergasted. She claps her hands. "They have a wonderful recreation program. A friend of mine is one of the therapists. Your date will be the fourteenth through the twenty-sixth. Here, I brought you a calendar, all filled in with details." She gives him a list of clothing he will need. "Look here, the camp bus will pick you up at ten in the morning. Nick, you're going to get out of the city during the hottest month of the year. What do you think of that?" She laughs, leans back to look at him.

What can he tell her? That Pearl's over daily, needing the key for her séance on the roof? That he's beginning to worry about Pearl's sanity? That August is his lucky month with the numbers? He could lose out on big money. Should he tell her Manny depends on him for a place to go? He stammers, but fear of authority renders him compliant as he recalls an old suspicion that, in some way, his nurse is connected to the Welfare Department and his social worker. Lack of cooperation might cause a collective rain of judgments to fall on his head.

It's evening before the bus of strangers reach Camp Recreate. Nick's room is narrow with one window at the far end. He looks out into the night. A single glaring lamp lights the parking lot. A terrible silence penetrates and he's unable to sleep. He struggles to place the electric fan on a metal chair where its shivering vibrations give him some comfort. He's wakened by the steady pattering of rain.

During breakfast the program director explains Project Recreate and they go off to assigned activity rooms. Everyone's color-coded into orange, green or blue teams. Nick's armband is orange. His activity room has an orange smiley face on the door. His recreational therapist reminds him of his nurse. She works hard at eye contact and is enthusiastic in spite of the rain. Campers are encouraged to hold and hug a little dog named Rx who retreats in terror. Four cats stride around, also part of therapy.

Nick's team makes nut cups for the party they will have on their last day. Bereft of words, Nick watches the others. When the rain stops he's taken for a boat ride. His life jacket does little to relieve his horror of water. He buys two post cards and can't think of a thing to tell Manny and Pearl. It becomes hard to remember their faces. By the third day he begins to feel he doesn't know who he is. He sits on the porch and watches the campers chasing Rx. Whooping with laughter, they turn over chairs and push each other to reach him. The little animal, eventually trapped, is snatched up and passed around to be petted. His body remains rigid as his eyes roll behind the hair that has escaped his pink ribbon. When they tire of him, he retreats to the dark corner behind Nick.

"What did your visitin' nurse have to say about you coming back a week early?" Manny asks, as Lewis shuffles the cards.

"Not much," Nick says.

"Pearl still coming to visit her dead pooch?"

"Not much anymore. She's pretty busy training her new dog. She changed his name to Rex. You know she can wear him around her neck like a fur piece? Gets away with it on subways."

"She never could a done that with that other dog," Manny says. "This one don't look like a rat." Lewis makes snapping gestures with his wrists as he deals and they watch.

Nick begins to pick up his cards and examines them. His nurse had been incredulous, her little mouth opening, her lips twitching as though forming words for the first time. "Wasn't it beautiful? Didn't you like the lake?"

He decided to tell her straight. "Yeah, there was trees and a lake, but I got homesick for Dyckman Street."

We Have Birds

YOU CAN see why it's hard keeping the place clean. I mean, they fly around. They were my son's, but when his wife wanted wall-to-wall, we got the birds. I would have closed the cage door (there are six of them and that's a lot of birds flying around), but the first time they buzzed my husband he said, "Ah," and (the bliss on his face) I knew I could never bring that look, even ten years ago. So I left the door open. They fly in formation just missing his head. Sometimes there is the barest brush of a wing.

My husband's a socialist, no longer card-carrying, but it never leaves you. You can understand; he has few pleasures.

He is also an educated man. I can only think of five, maybe six, times he's missed his weekly trip to the public library. He spends the entire evening, after an early supper. And book stores; he can't pass them by, not that he buys much, but in a busy store he can browse. No one minds.

Last year he floors me with early retirement. We never discussed it, so I just assumed, and then one day he says, "I put in for retirement." I couldn't even answer, just looked at him. By my open mouth he must have felt he had to explain. "You never know how long you have left," he said, and picked up his newspaper again, like he was pulling the curtain on act two.

I just sat there thinking. It's true, you never do know, but all the time I was wondering what he was going to do with all that time. More libraries? I'm not one to just accept things, but in this instance I felt it was something personal, and if he didn't want to talk about it, there was nothing to gain by hammering.

One day he came back from his book store browsing and says, "Leafing through the *Koran*, I find the Bedouins are on a par with the Philistines. They can be saved, but it's going to take a lot of work."

"What were you doing with the *Koran*?" I say.

He looks at me like maybe I hadn't really been listening. He will not repeat himself if he thinks that.

I rephrase my question. "What did you think of the *Koran*?"

"It's scold, scold, scold," he says and picks up his book. So, things go on this way.

I realize I'm not in this alone. My friends have relationship problems, some worse than others. Lorna, for instance, with her head for business. When she married Rodney he was about as sweet and insecure a man as anyone could find, but as he became successful, he became positively Germanic. Not only that, but Rodney outgrew appreciating Lorna's mother-instinct nature, which is the essence of Lorna. She should have married Harold Miller because, according to Shirley, that's what Harold's always wanting. Shirley won't have it. For instance, about ten years ago Harold went ice fishing with three buddies, on the lake, in the car. They drove to a likely spot and were thinking of setting up their equipment when someone noticed water coming through the bottom of the door. Well, three of them got out in a hurry, but Harold kept rattling around in back trying to find his thermos. The other three yelled at him to get out and finally he did. Just as he stepped on the ice the car shuddered, like it dreaded the plunge, and took it. That was in thirty feet of water. When they got back they all congregated in Shirley's living room to tell her about it. She told me how angry she was, but kept saying to herself, 'I'm not going to make mother-noises. That's what Harold's asking for.'

You just can't know what keeps people together or breaks them up. Take Ellie and Herb. They're divorced, but living together with a set of typewritten rules posted on the refrigerator. Ellie owns the house and when Herb breaks rules you should see the addendums. She says, "Keep this up and I won't renew your lease." He roars with laughter. Who knows if she means it?

I wouldn't enjoy that kind of relationship. I would like it if we could just talk like Stan Parr and Mara, yet Mara isn't too happy either. It annoys her that Stan is so casual about his elimination, going to the bathroom and leaving the door open so conversation isn't interrupted. She complains he has no modesty in that department, even in communal defecation on camping trips. She says, "It is as though the whole process is as natural as eating. Like an animal." Mara is a very delicate kind of person with sensitivity about anything brutish. She says, "I've always been constipated, myself."

One of Louise's greatest comforts had been to contemplate Larry's helplessness after she died. She knew this to be mean and beneath her, but couldn't help savoring a kind of revenge. It was not to be. When Louise died, Larry, snug on the eighth floor of a retirement complex, had to beat away cookie-bearing ladies of that establishment. He rises late, taxies to lunch, returns to read or write and evenings he's the minority male in the dining hall, holding forth at a table with seven women.

I am reflecting on this when my husband comes in with three library books. I look at the titles. "Interesting," I say.

"Too bad you don't have someone to share."

"If you want to go out for Chinese," he says, "I could give you a summary of two thousand years of Chinese history." He smiles as the birds buzz him.

I snap the fresh water tubes on their cage. "Yes," I say, "That would be nice."

The Poetry Evening

I WAS fifteen when I decided to harden my heart to Father. It was either that or more hurt. I would shut him out and I started by cutting my hair.

It was to be one of his poetry evenings and I could imagine the adoring cluster of females arranging themselves at his feet. Oh, there would be a scattering of men, hardly lovers of poetry, but sulking, shifting-footed men who joined their ladies only to see what Father was up to.

He had been up to rehearsing all day, marching the beach. From the house I saw him intoning his verses, arms flailing, scattering gulls. He was back at lunch, voice ripened to perfect pitch, lip in shape, hair a wild curling mass. I snapped dusty rugs over the porch rail, letting it all drift down on him. The sun snagged squint-blue from his eyes as he opened his arms to me. He would send up some ode or sonnet, but I was in before it came to him.

"I hate his poetry evenings," I stormed, slamming the door.

"Why? You used to love them," Mother said, thrusting the end of a curtain rod my way. She began threading the rod. "Your father even had you recite."

"Before I got so big and ugly."

"Oh, Mara, no."

"Oh yes. I remember him telling you once that I reminded him of a heron trying to get off the ground and once he said it wouldn't be long before I heaped that final indignity on him by making him a grandfather. That's exactly what he said."

"He didn't mean it that way. I think he's just afraid of getting old, of not doing the things he's dreamed of."

Mother's face, soft with sympathy, enraged me. She put a hand on my arm, but I shook it off. "It's rather sad, Mara. All those poems lying in his file. He says it's like leaving his footprints in the snow."

"So he trots off to leave footprints on the beach, leaving all the work to us. All the cleaning, the baking, all for his poetry evening."

Mother sighed and took the hanger from me. "Try to understand your father, Mara."

"Understand?" I snapped, feeling her reproach, "I understand. I see through him. I know what these poetry evenings are all about and he can't stand that."

Mother's voice, taut as a wire, came flat and smooth. "What do you mean?"

From below, Father called. "Ellie, something smells good. When do we eat?"

In that strained moment, as we looked at each other, I realized I was taller than Mother. My voice, new to me, surged in a rage that excited me to slash at her. "You had better go, Mother. The master calls. He's had a hard day on the beach."

"Mara. I am not joking. Tell me what you mean."

Frightened, wanting to take it back, I heard my little-girl voice. "It's just that every time he has a poetry evening, well, like tonight it's Lew Sarett's work, but not entirely. Sandwiched right in between his poems, Father will insert some of his own." Her face was unchanged. Only her eyes moved as they probed my face. "He always does it," I went on. "Everyone knows it and it's not hard to tell which is which if you're half awake."

Her chuckle erupted. Relieved, I continued. "Father knows his own poetry by heart, for one thing, so he can really concentrate on his delivery. And he watches everyone, even with his eyes rolled up in his head he doesn't miss a thing. Then some idiot squeals, 'how moving, oh, that's the best,' and of course, he has to confess it's his and they all say they can't believe it and Father looks like a damned fool."

Mother was laughing when Father sang out, "Ellie,–Ellie–."

Responding in kind, she called, "Coming,–coming,–coming," and she practically threw herself down the stairs to present his lunch.

Like Vachel Lindsay, Father wrote most of his poetry while walking or to music. When I was little I would sometimes waken, wrapped up in Daddy's robe and listening on the landing. The language was beautiful, even though I didn't understand.

It was at the time he stopped writing poetry that he started his poetry evenings. I begged him to keep writing, but he laughed, "a man has to be in love to write poetry." I didn't want him to stop because he worked on the walking part with me. I was quite young, for I remember having to almost run to keep up. If he had a line he didn't want to lose I had to keep that in my head until we got home. I'd repeat it over and over. Mother was right. We had been close. Little by little it all changed. Somehow it seemed I irritated him if I wasn't his adoring little girl.

Daddy had always liked my hair and often touched it as he passed. More and more I was plunking myself down in his path, just for that touch. Still, we battled. It was after one of these scenes, when we yelled at each other and Mother flew back and forth between us like a torn dove, that I decided to pursue a life of science. I became as visible as possible in this pursuit. Bottles of insects lay about and I boiled the meat off the skulls of dead birds and animals and left them on tables and shelves. He seemed to take no notice. One morning, as he sat for breakfast, I was dissecting an earthworm on the kitchen table.

"You find this interesting, Mara?" he asked with distaste.

"Very."

"What is that thing?"

"It's an earthworm. Here, you can see how he strains waste through this tube and that's his nerve cord and that's the central gut."

"Well, get that thing off my table."

"It's not a thing," I snapped. "It's a *lumbricus terrestris*."

"It doesn't even have a brain," he pronounced. "A life unexamined is not worth living."

Mother came laughing from the kitchen, carrying his breakfast tray. "Who said that? Plato?"

"Can't you be original about anything?" I shouted.

He laughed.

"The whole world would die without earthworms!" I screamed, afraid I might cry.

He continued to laugh, circling an arm around Mother to guide her to the terrace with his tray. "I tell you, Ellie, we should put this Sarah Hartbern on the stage. She's far too emotional for science."

On Lew Sarett night I kept out of the front room, but I could hear Father as Mother and I worked in the kitchen. We were starting to pay attention so we could tell when the cheese muffins should be heated. I opened the kitchen door a crack. The dark resonance of his voice moved over me.

"You measure time to me like a chemist. On the stroke I hear you, booted, wearing the mask."

The words flowed to where we perspired by the oven. Mother stared at the door. "What is he reciting? That's not Sarett."

"No. I hate it. I can't–"

"Shush," she said. "I want to hear it." She stood by the door, absently drying her hands on a towel. "He didn't tell me he was writing again."

Father's voice seemed torn from his throat. "If I would love I must dare to face my fall. In madness I flung my colors, Van Gogh gone mad. You caught my hand and held it to your tears–"

"I can't stand to listen to that junk," I cried, running up the back stairs to the bathroom. I glared hatefully at myself in the mirror and seizing the scissors, hacked off my hair. Now, all of me was ugly.

Walking to the front stairs, I slowly descended into the living room. Amid the accolade of applause over his poem, Father saw me. His eyes flicked wide a moment before he laughed. "Behold, Mara. A rag, a bone, and a hank of hair." There was a soft flutter of laughter.

I did not look at him, but walked into the kitchen. Mother gasped, "Mara, your hair." She put her arms around me and began to cry.

From the front room we could hear the last of Lew Sarett's poem.

> "Step softly, March, with your rampant hurricane;
> Nuzzling one another, and whimpering with pain,
> The new little foxes are shivering in the rain–
>   Step softly."

Dining with Anita and Morris

ANITA AND Morris have been fighting. I sense it the moment we enter. Their voices strain in greeting, her hug's edgy with the energy of battle. I glance at my husband who's acknowledging the aroma oozing from the kitchen. He reaches down to rub the cat and I love him for his innocence. "Hello Kitty," Roger says, "How's the world treating you?"

Although Anita and Morris have been our friends for forty years, they sit and face us with stiff backs and bent knees. The usual inquiries, concerning health and the current activities of our far-flung kids, get passed around several times before Morris lurches to his feet to get his tidy little tray of drinks. All the drinks are different and in different glasses and Morrie doesn't need to tell me the Rhine wine is on my left. He passes Roger's Scotch and Roger thanks him, saying something to the effect that all needs are met in this household. Morrie's response is a cold, "Really?" That's not Morrie and I'm becoming nervous.

We sip and chat and I feel the awkwardness between us, the tension in the room. Morris remembers the hors d'oeuvres and bolts to the kitchen. Anita is suddenly removing plates and cutlery for two settings. "We were having Shirley and Ben," she explains, "but we canceled them."

"Canceled them?"

"Morris's idea," Anita says, compressing her lips as though she must say no more. She disappears into the kitchen.

"Why would they cancel Shirley and Ben?" I ask Roger.

"Not enough food?" he laughs, thinking he's cute.

"They've been fighting," I say.

"What?"

"Anita and Morris have been fighting."

"Nonsense," he says, bending to talk to the cat. "No discord in Kitty's household. No sir, Kitty won't have it."

I find it exasperating the way Roger shrugs off any of my perceptions.

Morris returns with the hors d'oeuvres and Anita sits in the chair farthest from me, an unnatural gesture since we usually tire of man-talk and carry on a private conversation.

"I trust Ben's not having fibrillations again," I say, hoping to learn why they were canceled.

"No," Morris says. "We'll discuss that after dinner."

I've been saving what I think is a hilarious story about my younger sister and her Asian boyfriend. Though Sheilah is committed to him, she holds back her favors with Puritan reserve, allowing him to lead her through a flowery courtship. This is so unlike the Sheilah I used to know, who once danced unabashed to Bolero on a restaurant's table top. I begin my story, and in moments, realize no one is listening.

Morris finishes his drink and says, "Shall we eat?" We move to the table and he and Anita bring in dishes and begin to serve. "This man is Chinese if I remember correctly," Morris says.

"Yes," I say. "They both lost spouses early in life. My sister became interested in Buddhism many years ago. That's how they met. He's a little older, probably my age. It's really a rather lovely relationship."

"How's that?" Morris asks.

I explain it's the tradition that's followed. Sheilah feels

secure because of tradition. She knows each step of the way. Knows what to expect from marriage. It frees her to think about her work.

"Exactly," Morris says. He wipes his mouth and looks at me. "What are your opinions of infidelity in marriage?"

I wonder if this has something to do with Ben and Shirley and don't care to discuss their problems, so I flippantly say, "You mean affairs like Chester Stone and Phyllis Danbritz?"

Both Roger and Morris are stunned and I'm pleased that Anita and I share this information.

Morris leans towards me. "Phyllis Danbritz with Chester Stone?"

"The same," I say.

"But why?" Roger cries. "Phyllis was so..." He searches for a word to describe her lack of grace or beauty and finally expresses distaste with a twist of his lips. "Chester's wife was a knockout."

"You noticed, did you?" Morris retorts.

Of course Roger doesn't react. He's still incredulous. "But when would they?" he persists. "Chester's wife never worked."

"Saturdays, her super market day," Anita says. "When she roared away in her little Volkswagen, Chester slipped, no galoped, across the road to Phyllis." For the first time Anita seems herself and I begin to relax, but I see the lawyer in Morris at work. He can't imagine Chester with the president of the PTA, the neighborhood organizer, the McGovern champion who beat us all into back-breaking hours of volunteer work. "Not Phyllis Danbritz," he says. "I can't picture it."

"I can," Anita says. "Did you ever meet Chester's mother? No? Well Phyllis was exactly like Chester's mother. She would direct everything in that relationship. 'Just your slacks, Chester. Don't take your shirt off. There isn't time.'" She laughs and I join her, happy to share.

Roger begins to choke.

"For heaven's sakes, Roger, chew your food," I say and explain he's always wolfed his food, but lately his swallowing can't keep up with the food presented and he chokes. We wait for his spasm to subside and I tell them his doctor feels age has slowed peristalsis and Roger should chew more and slow down, but nothing will change Roger's habits.

"My new doctor thinks I have a hiatal hernia," Roger says defensively. "It has nothing to do with chewing. She said she wanted to have tests, but I told her I wanted no invasive procedures and no drugs. I always tell a new doctor that. X-rays, O.K. This new doctor is very nice. Respects my wishes, doesn't try to talk me into anything."

"In other words, nothing is accomplished," Morris snorts.

"I wouldn't say that," Roger says. "I think it's important to arrive at an understanding with your doctor. Marva Ketterling, that's my new doctor, is very well qualified and she looks healthy. I like that in a doctor. Dr. Stone just didn't give me confidence. He had a face like bread dough."

"For God's sakes, Roger, he's been on dialysis," Anita says, lifting the meat platter. "Have some more meat." She begins scraping a slice of lamb on my plate as though propelling it into the garbage. She knows I eat very little meat.

"Pass the mint jelly to your wife," Morris says.

"To your wife?" I say. "What's this 'to your wife' business? All this unnatural talk and attention. You're like parents damming an anger flood with bags of words. What's wrong? What's going on with you two?"

Roger is appalled. Anita and Morris look at me dumbly.

"I'm asking," I say. "Damn it, I've got rights. You've been our dear friends half a lifetime."

"Go ahead, tell them," Morris says. His voice has a cutting force that matches the hard lines around his mouth. I can imagine him in court and would not like to be in a fight with this man. I look at Anita and give her a sympathetic look, but she lowers her head. "After dinner," she says.

Dinner is a silent affair except for Roger's episodes of choking. I try another light anecdote. "Some of the fellows at the recycling station are giving me a hard time. Do you have trouble, Anita?" She shakes her head. "They yell at me like, 'Lady, you can't put green glass in with brown.'" I project my voice, as they do, and it startles everyone. "Yesterday it was because there was a stray tissue in with miscellaneous paper. 'Hey lady, come pick that out!'"

Roger starts his teasing mode. "So why are you having all these problems? Anita's not."

"Anita probably flirts," Morris responds. "She's always dressed for seduction."

"What are you talking about?" Anita snaps. "Your global generalizations really annoy me, Morris. Examples, please."

"Remember that fake fur dress? Short, my god it was short, cut up to here."

"That was the sixties. That was the style!"

"Can you believe we wore things that short?" I say. "I remember that dress. I hate the little-girl look these days."

"It's the sixties all over again," Anita says. "That fake fur had a zipper all the way down the front. We were in Chicago for some reason, some affair, I can't remember, but Saul Bellow was ogling me from across the room."

Morris leans across the table. "Really? I don't remember that."

"Well, I do," I say. "Saul Bellow was teaching at the University of Chicago and you two were at some big publisher party and Anita goofed her chance to talk to him."

"What a memory," Anita says with admiration.

"Who could forget that? Saul Bellow eyeing you."

Anita laughs. She's pleased. "He was, he was. Today I would have gone over and introduced myself and told him how much I liked *Augie March*. It would be nice to be able to say I talked with Saul Bellow, but I didn't have the nerve."

"But, Saul Bellow," I say.

"He was already on his third wife. It was the dress. I could see that. Men were just magnetized by it."

"You had a good figure."

"I was forty."

"You were at your peak at forty," Morris says.

Anita sits back in her chair, musing. "It was something about the fake fur. I could see men looking at it. They wanted to reach out and touch it. I've always regretted not going over and saying I admired his work. He'd written *Augie March* by then. I don't think I ever read anything else of his."

"I have *The Magic Barrel* if you want to read some of his short stories," Roger offers, but Anita's flat tone indicates she already has too much to read. A long silence follows and we take our chairs to the other room. Anita chooses an armchair and pulls a throw-quilt around her as though she's cold. In moments, Kitty climbs onto her lap. They make a lovely picture, woman and cat. Anita's heavy gray hair is pulled back severely from a face that needs no distracting curls.

Morris is boiling, though he keeps his composure. "Jan," he

says, "I'm probably the only one who didn't know about this, so I apologize if you don't know about Anita and Roger."

I have no idea why I smile. I'm aware I have a foolish grin on my face, that my heart is hammering so loud I hear pulsations in my ears.

"You know, then. How long have you known?" His voice is run-down.

"Know what?" I say.

"Know about their affair."

"Affair?" I turn to look at Roger, who's open-mouthed. I laugh, it's so absurd.

"Oh, not now," Morris says. "It's over now, but it happened. We've been deceived."

I look at Anita, who has wrapped the throw quilt tighter around her body. Only her face and the top of her head are visible. Kitty is a mere bulge. I can't see Roger without turning around again and I refuse to do that.

Morris stands and begins to pace. It takes several moments of limping before his bad hip will allow smooth movement. "Only yesterday," he says, "only yesterday did I learn of this when I came across an old love letter from Roger."

"Love letter from Roger? That hurts. He's never written me a love letter."

"I was too young," Roger says. "I couldn't even spell."

"You could have used a dictionary," I say.

"The point is, we've been deceived," Morris says. "They have been living a lie. They don't love us at all."

"That's not true and you know it," Anita says.

Morris stands over us. "I think Jan and I deserve an explanation of some sort. Don't you, Anita?"

"I suppose," she says.

"Well?"

Anita's arm escapes the blanket and waves at Roger. "Go ahead."

"I can't remember," he says.

For a moment she doesn't speak. I see the coloring of rage. "You don't remember?"

"It was years ago."

"So was my eighth grade graduation, but I remember!"

"You explain then," Roger says, "you initiated it."

"I did not."

"You did."

"Stop it, you two. We're getting nowhere," Morris yells. He looks at me. "They don't love us at all."

"Of course we do," Roger says, his voice miserable.

"I think we'd better go," I say and begin rocking motions to get out of the low chair. "Will someone help me out of this damned chair?"

"You can't go," Anita says. "Morris made a cheesecake."

I give up the struggle. Morris makes a fantastic cheesecake. Years ago he gave me the recipe, but I could see it would take all day so I've never tried it. I study the rug. I'm unsure how a wronged person should act. After a long silence I say, "How did it happen?"

"How did it happen?" Morris barks.

"What were the circumstances? Had it been building up for a long time? Were they both unhappy at home?" My questions heat me up, give me focus. I forget the cheesecake and look at Anita.

"Morris and I were having troubles," she says in a low voice. "We'd been to a marriage counselor, but you know Morrie. Can't face personal problems. On our first visit he spent fifty minutes telling the counselor his concept of time. I'm not exaggerating.

Fifty minutes. So, finally he went to visit his sister and then... then the kitchen drain wouldn't work."

"So you called Roger?"

"Yes."

"Was he able to fix it?"

"No."

"Ha!" I say and turn to give Roger a triumphant look. He couldn't fix a bent paper clip.

"What were we having troubles about?" Morris asks.

Anita scratches her head and adjusts the position of the cat. "I think it had something to do with the war, about the amount of time I was spending for peace."

"I remember," I say. "You and I were working with draft resisters. Also, making leaflets. Roger complained about late suppers, but you said Morris was fed up."

"What a time," Anita sighs, "What a time. Remember petitioning door to door? You took one side of the street and I did the other. Remember the hostility? Sometimes we'd just meet at the end of a block and cry. Do you think you could ever go through that now?"

"Never," I say. "You have to be resilient, like your Rachel."

Anita finishes her drink. "Oh, God love her, I don't know how she does it with three kids."

"Ladies!" Morris interjects. "You're getting off the subject."

Anita and I both arch eyebrows and assume identical posturing. "Not ladies...WOMEN," we snap. There's a collective groan from the men.

"How long did this affair last?" I ask.

"Not long," Anita says. "I stopped it soon after Morris came back."

"You stopped it?" Roger says. "I stopped it."
"You did not."
"I did."

Hot for battle, Anita throws off her blanket and leans forward. "You did not! Morris, get the letter. It proves I put an end to it, regretted it from the start."

Standing as though addressing a court, Morris fumbles in his pocket, holds the letter before him. "My darling I beg of you, don't leave me in this cruel way."

"There," Anita says. "Conclusive evidence."

"Nothing of the sort," Roger protests. "We had twenty or thirty such partings. Most of them were mine."

"Twenty or thirty?" I choke.

"I remember exactly the last time," Anita shouts. "It was after Roger'd hung my drapes."

"He hung your drapes?" I cry. "The blue ones you used to have in the living room?"

"Yes," Anita says.

I turn to Roger. "How many times, how many times did I have to beg you to help me with ours?"

Anita sweeps Kitty from her lap and rises with an energy I haven't seen in years. "You were a disappointment from the start," she rages. "The only affair of my life and it had to be you."

Roger looks devastated. "You needn't be cruel," I say.

"Jan, what do you have to say?" Morris asks.

"Say?"

"Yes. What are you thinking? Right this moment, what are your thoughts?"

"Actually, it crossed my mind that if I'd known this when it happened, I would have lost everything. I was so self-righteous in those days. I wouldn't have had Anita to pull me through the mastectomy nightmare, I would have lost Roger and our best years. I love you all," my voice croaks and I begin rocking motions to get out of my chair. "I think we'd better go."

"Wait," Morris says. He leaves the room and Kitty decides to try my lap. We sit. Morris returns with the cheesecake. He holds it before him and we murmur praises before he cuts it. "I, for one, am glad to have this over and I intend to put it all behind me," he says, looking like a man who has won a case in court. Anita gives him an affectionate smile. I turn to Roger. Wiping tears, he gives me a brave little smile. In silence we continue to consume the cheesecake until Roger begins choking.

"What am I going to do with him?" I ask Anita. "He won't chew."

"Put everything in a blender. Make him drink it."

"I've never had a blender."

"I'll give you mine. I used to fix malts for the kids, but I never use it anymore."

We're both pleased with the plan. We smile and return to the cake.

Jari

"OH, I do thoroughly dislike hearing the word 'Pa,'" Mother said, even before telling me that Eban Vahatalo had called to say his Pa was coming to town and could I go to the matinee with him.

I always liked Eban, but after school farm kids had chores, and friendships didn't build up easily. When I close my eyes, I see him then tow-headed, hair too long and so fine it floated around his head. He was never tall, but squarish like the Finns, Mother said, and sure of himself. Eban walked sure of himself.

I told Eban I'd meet him at Daddy's hardware and we saw a Gene Autry picture. Afterwards, Daddy brought us home for ice cream.

"Didn't I see some sheep lying dead in your south pasture?" Daddy asked.

Eban was licking his spoon. "There was two," he said.

I saw mother wince at his grammar.

"Dog packs?" Daddy asked.

Eban laid his spoon on the tablecloth. "No, Pa don't sell old ewes when they quit birthin'. The price's not worth the bother. He puts 'em to pasture and when they die he lets 'em lie there a while, maybe twelve to eighteen hours and then you just scrape the wool off without no problem. We just put the wool in a bag and wait until shearing time and put it in with the rest."

Daddy was dishing more ice cream into Eban's bowl.

"Pa don't waste nothin'," Eban said. "He boils up the carcass, bones and all, and cooks it down for the hogs."

Mother gave me a significant look. I was delighted.

In high school Eban asked me to a dance. I remember his truck coming up our drive, its frame lacy as a valentine from winter salt.

"Good lord," Daddy said.

"Don't judge him by his truck," I said.

"Honey," Daddy said, "I'm not judging him. The truck's not safe if the rest of it's that rusted out. I'm afraid you'll fall through the floor boards."

It wasn't a good start. Even my best friend said, "Eban's father is a mean man. Don't get tied up with Finns."

After high school I worked as a secretary in Chicago and forgot about Eban until I met him two and a half years later, in such an accidental way, I wonder at how close I came to never finding him.

A bunch of us girls went to Frandy's Road House for supper. We were eating and watching the dancers when Eban came in with friends. Pretty soon they were cutting in on the dancers and when Eban swung this girl by I willed him to look my way and he just lifted his eyes and searched me out in the shadows. Afterwards he walked over, sure of himself, and asked me to dance. Later he separated me from my friends and said he would take me home. I liked the way he handled his truck This one had seats so wide four could sit side by side. We parked by the lake and he turned off the lights and motor and reached for me as though everything was understood.

I quit my Chicago job and started working for E&H White. It felt good to be back in Ishpeming. After Chicago and some of the men I'd known there, it felt good to be pursued by Eban Vahatalo.

Daddy said, "It's not that I don't think he can take care of you. He's built up that farm. Got some prize Hereford stock and he's smart not risking everything on one breed. I've seen belted Galloway and Aberdeen Angus on his place. The trouble, I see, is you'd be moving into a man's world. Their women all died off."

"That's no accident," Mother said. "They expect women to work right out in the field, like a man, even when they're pregnant."

"You'd be stuck out there," my best friend said.

"I have a job in town," I reminded her.

"And what about when the babies come?"

"What if there aren't any?" I said.

We didn't have a honeymoon because of seasonal work, but I didn't care. My boss gave me a week's leave and I used it to fix up Eban's four-room trailer before going back to work. It was parked under four huge pines in his Daddy's yard.

Five days after the wedding, I invited Eban's father to supper. He came across the yard in a fresh shirt with a string tie and his walk, so like Eban, I had to blink to make sure it was Jari Vahatalo. Eban put him at the head of the table and as soon as the two men sat I could see they were ready to eat.

"You married at a good time," Jari said. "Lambin's coming up pretty quick now. I see the udders filling. Maybe only a week or so. The Missus might as well get broke in."

I was clearing the table and I just stared at him. "That's right," he said.

"Me?"

"You. You gotta get started on lambin' some time. Might as well be now."

The first thing I felt was anger. He was so sure of himself pouring more coffee and turning to talk to Eban as though everything was settled.

"I don't know the first thing about it," I said.

He turned to look at me. "I know that," he said. His face mild.

"Besides," I said, almost laughing, feeling this was ridiculous, that I had misunderstood something, "I already have a full time job at E&H White."

His face was tolerant, almost kindly, as though speaking to a child. "You're just going to have to kiss E&H White goodbye."

"But I can't. Eban, tell him."

"You're family now," Jari said softly. "This here's family business. Eban does cows and beef. You and I do sheep. Them sheep are gonna be yours when I'm gone. Eban can't keep up with it. Now you come through with some husky boys and you're free to dilly dally with E&H White all you want." He smiled and rose to leave. "You do a nice table, Missus. Much obliged."

When Eban came up from the barn that evening I was all ready for him, but with his kissing and his explanations that it wasn't hard except the lambing, the shearing being done by professionals who only had to be fed the one day, and that it would be a business for our boys, and that what I earned at E&H White was nothing compared to sheep, it seemed the most logical thing in the world until Mother phoned the next morning.

"Missus, you in there?" Jari called.

I opened the door, ready to tell him I planned to visit Mother.

"Get your work duds on and come on down to the pen. Things are going to happen pretty quick now."

Booted, churning with resentment, kicking tufts of grass, I hurried to where the woven wire fence held the sheep. Jari sat on a stump drinking coffee. "Here, I brought you a cup. Pour yourself coffee and sit while I explain things."

I poured my coffee, standing over him.

"Look under that first 'un's tail. She's 'bout ready. See how she's bulging and wet? Restless too."

I walked around. They all looked ready to me. "What am I supposed to do if they all start coming at once and you're busy?" I shouted. I gulped coffee to steady myself.

I heard Eban's laugh. "You scaring her to death, Pa? I come down the hill and see her concentrating like she's going to fly the space shuttle all by herself."

Eban put his hand on my shoulder. "I came over to help. Got more coffee, Pa?"

"Plenty. There's a cup on the fence post."

"Is everything going to happen at once?" I asked.

"Just about," Eban said. "Gestation's 150 days from when Pa puts a buck with the ewes."

"One buck?" I said. "There must be fifty sheep."

"If he's young, one buck can service that many," Jari said, taking off his cap to massage his scalp. "I plan birthin' for April.

I like having green grass when there's lambin'. Always hated lambin' in a cold barn with a lantern and having to worry it's going to be freezing." Jari was doing another tour of inspection and called out to me. "Green grass about an inch high and lambin' right out in the warm fields is best. Now Fred Purdy, he got to get the jump on everybody. He's like some old woman getting' out her Monday wash. Last year he lost a third of his lambs to pneumonia and scours because he had 'em in March and we got that cold snap. He'll breed 'em early too. The man's just born impatient."

"Pa doesn't breed them until they're two years old," Eban explained. "Makes birthing easier."

The men grew silent, intent. Jari sat on his stump looking out across fields as though listening. I glanced at Eban staring into his coffee with the same concentration. I could feel expectation, the silence of ewes, and then a beginning thump of restless hooves.

"They're startin'," Jari said, moving from the stump.

"Put these on and stay by Pa," Eban said, handing me rubber gloves that reached my elbows. He moved off among the animals.

"We don't do nothin' unless they need help," Jari said, and in moments the birthing began.

I moved and watched. Several times I saw Jari assist, and though he explained, I was deaf to human sound. I saw one lamb unattended. Its mother seemed lost in solitary reverie as she faced the barn. Nudging Jari, I pointed to the lamb.

"Remember where it is," he said and when another ewe labored he sent me for the lamb. Jari held the ewe's head to keep her from looking around, his grip light as she labored. When her lamb dropped, his arm tightened, strained to hold her. Eyes rolling, she struggled to turn her head. "Rub your lamb in the afterbirth," Jari gasped, his breath heaving as he pressed his head against her face. I hurried. The ewe's impatience threatened her newborn with stamping hooves. When released she looked over the lambs, smelled them and accepted both.

"We was lucky," Jari said. "It don't always work."

By the time we finished there were two rejected lambs needing a mother. We took them to Jari's house and rubbed them with towels. In a few minutes he had their bottles ready. "Both females," he said. "Hope you can save 'em. Here, you feed and I'll get supper goin'."

"Eyes as big as saucers," Eban laughed as he entered. You see her, Pa? Eyes big as saucers."

I handed Eban one of the bottles, but he shook his head. "They have to know you're their ma," he said. "You fixing to feed us, Pa?"

"Had it in mind," Jari said, frying up potatoes and ham.

"Are they all delivered?" I asked.

"Nope, I'll bed down near the stragglers soon as I fix me a bite."

"It's two a.m. Is your clock right?" I asked.

"That's the way time goes on a farm," Jari said. He poured glasses of milk. "I worked for a man named Bill Curdy who had four hundred sheep and I did everything around. When the lambs were a few days old, I docked their tails and castrated the whole lot. Took all day. Course only about half of them needed castratin', but there was four hundred tails." He looked over at my lambs. "Them two's taking good to your feedin'. I sat on a stool the whole day dockin' tails with a sharp knife and after castratin' I give them to Curdy's young boy who put them with their dam. She took care of 'em. You don't want to wait until they're too old. The older they get the harder it is on 'em, besides you want to get it over before fly season. A fly will lay eggs on any kind of wound and the maggots clean it up good, but they don't stop there. They'll go right on eatin' good flesh. Help yourself to coffee, Missus."

Eban poured my coffee from the thermos and filled his daddy's cup.

"When I castrated I did it by bitin' off the testicles. Now you might wonder how anyone can do that, but it was just raw meat. No bleedin' to mention and didn't take any time at all. Only once did I have one bleed enough to die."

"Ellie here's got a good sharp bite," Eban said. "Show Pa your teeth, Ellie."

I jumped up and the men laughed.

"He's jokin' you, missus. We use emasculators now. No rubber bands or primitive doings on this farm."

"Why do you even bother?" I asked. "Is a little lamb going to attack you like a bull?"

"No, but castrated they gain faster to the meat cuts," Jari said. "And the tails got to be short or they hang down below a sheep's vent. Makes for dampness and soil and a sweet place for maggots if the tail's not docked. Also it's easier to breed a ewe if her tail's not in the way." He looked at my lambs. "Them two look pretty content. Come on and eat."

Eban and I put the lambs together in one bed. "I'm going to name them Jody and Penny," I said.

"She's named them, Pa," Eban called out to his daddy.

Jari was dumping his fried supper on our plates. He grinned at his son. "I knew she was going to work out just fine."

Before we went to the stake-out Eban glued cotton to the end of my barrel sight, saying, "That's to help you aim in the dark. Sometimes it's pretty hard to know where the end of your gun's pointing."

"Thanks," I said as I pulled on a sweater. Eban set the gun by the door and I picked up the thermos. "You know you don't have to do this," he said.

"I want to."

"It's going to be a long night," Eban said, putting his arms around me. I held my provisions between us. "I'll carry the gun," he said, picking it up and opening the door.

The sheep were in a massive mesh wire pen with the car parked in the middle. I could see Jari up front. He had thrown a pillow and sleeping bag in back for me.

"Try and get some sleep," Eban said. "The sheep will let you know when the dogs come. They'll set the fence to twanging. Now, take your time. Remember, you don't have to shoot if you don't want to."

I nodded, wanting to go home with him, but hugging my thermos. I watched Eban start up the hill towards our trailer and I climbed in back and slammed the car door.

It was dark, but I could see Jari's head and shoulders. I began to arrange my sleeping bag.

"I figure they'll come from the east," Jari said, "so I've set my gun up on the right hand side, ready to go."

I acknowledged his statement by laying the barrel of my gun on the open window sill.

"If they come from the west they would have had to pass my place and they likely know better than that, but if they do come from the west, be careful of changing sides with that loaded gun. You could blow my head clean off," he laughed. "Everyone would agree it was a natural accident, but I suspect you would always wonder."

"What do you mean?" I said.

Jari pounded his pillow into shape and disappeared as he lay down on the seat. "You figure Jody would be alive if I'd let her stay in your yard?"

I didn't answer.

"It figures," he said. "Miracle is she lived at all. Now that Penny, I knew she'd make it."

"Jody wasn't like Penny," I said. "When they'd see me with the bottles they'd both come running. Penny headed straight for her bottle, but Jody wanted me. Even with the nipple in her mouth she'd turn until her little rump pressed against me."

"It's woman's nature to be taken in by the helpless," Jari said. "That's why women do best with sheep." I didn't respond. "Did you know sheep have the least will to live of any farm animal? Once down, they just refuse to live. When they get pneumonia they're the sorriest looking thing you ever want to see. They get this hang-dog look and then start this pitiful huffin' and puffin'. I always try chopped carrots and apples. Even rolled oats with molasses and lettuce. I remember Eban, once, using soda crackers and it worked. I'm sure it's the pamperin' saves 'em."

"Jody wasn't ready to be in the fields with the others," I said. "I could hear her calling me. I wanted to get her, but Eban wouldn't let me. He always does what you say, but I say I saved her so she was mine."

"She had to learn sheep ways. If you wait too long they never learn."

"So what good was it having the dogs get her?"

"It's natural, you grieving her."

"I'm not grieving. I'll do that after I kill the dogs."

It was quiet for a time and I wondered if he'd fallen asleep.

"Missus, you're too keen on killing. I wish I could get you to see they're just plain old farm dogs bandin' together, like boys in the tavern, going out to have themselves a little fun. Generally they'll run sheep, not to eat and kill, but just to have themselves a time. Course running sheep can overheat 'em to death so no farmer blames you for shooting his dog. I don't know what got into them dogs this time. One of 'em must a lost his head and started the killing. I've never had it happen like this before."

"It's not just Jody," I said. Jari was quiet. I watched clouds racing past the moon. "I liked my job. I miss talking with women."

Jari sighed. "Sometimes I don't see things too good." There was a twang of fencing and he sat up. "If they're coming, it's awful early." He sat silent for several minutes, but the sheep seemed calm. "I see you had a girlfriend visiting you. Did you have a good visit?"

"No," I said, "it wasn't good." I heard Jari lying down. "I served her coffee and sweet rolls in the living room, but she couldn't stomach eating with the lamb pen in the kitchen." I paused, remembering Roberta's face. "When she left I walked her to her car and when she got in she kept sniffing and turning her foot to inspect her shoe." I laughed, remembering Roberta's fussy little movements. Jari chuckled.

"She asked me to go out to lunch with her and I explained that I had to feed the lambs. She said, 'You just have to put your foot down. Don't let them take advantage of you.' I thought she meant you and Eban, but she was talking about the lambs." Jari and I both began to laugh and when we stopped, one of us would start up again.

"Eban's going to think we got a bottle down here," Jari said. "And we won't have no dogs show up for our trouble."

We quieted. I thought he had fallen asleep and I pulled my sleeping bag up against the chill.

"I like them blackface sheep," Jari said, his voice dreamy like Eban's in the night. "The face an' head an' ears are jet black with no wool on 'em. Same with the legs. The bucks got that Roman nose, no horns, and they can get to be a hundred seventy to two hundred pounds. They're big fellows."

"What kind are they?"

"Suffolk. I plan to get some started someday. I fancy havin' a couple of Karakuls. That's a fur-bearing sheep." Jari sat up and looked over the back of the seat. "You heard of Persian lamb coats? That's where they come from. I just want to raise a couple. You know, Missus, they was started way back before the time of Christ, over in Russia and Afghanistan, up in the mountains near the Caspian Sea. I seen 'em once at a fair. The fleece on the lamb was curly-tight, and its dam had hair hanging long, clear to the ground. They shear 'em for carpet wool. Wouldn't it just be nice having a couple of them hanging around here? Course I like our Oxfords, but it would be fun having a sheep that goes way back in history like that."

He stopped talking to listen. "What's that?" I asked.

"Sheep are stamping their feet. Dogs are coming from somewhere. Get ready." We heard the twang of the wire mesh fence. "That's sheep rubbing against the fence." I could see him sighting his raised gun. "Here they come. Four or five of 'em."

"That's the white collie from up the road," I said.

"Lie down, Missus. You don't want to do this."

I threw myself down waiting for the two shots that followed. Eban was running down the hill when we got out of the car. "There's a German shepherd up there and I see you got Sorenson's collie."

"He was leadin' the pack," Jari said. "I think we're over dog problems." I stood staring at the dog and leaned against

Eban when his arm circled my shoulders. "Damned shame," Jari said. "He was a beauty." Jari began digging. "Damn, I'm hungry. I've got pie on the table and we can have ice cream on top. Why don't you go up and make the coffee and me an' Eban will be finished with this in a jiffy."

I went slowly to his house to begin preparations. I'd left my thermos in the car and started back to get it. The rhythmical thrusts of the shovels sang out, and above this I heard Jari's voice. "Naw, she couldn't kill nobody's dog. It wouldn't be natural. She's gonna grieve awhile. You gotta expect that, but what do you think if maybe I get her a pair of them Karakuls, just for her own? She could keep them up in your yard."

Mr. Karas

I OFTEN assigned a student to Mr. Karas, though my rationale's unsound. He does most of his own care, but he's without family, not entertained by television, and he enjoys students. The elderly man's a fixture here; both legs weighted with the hardware of external fixation. He should have been independent on crutches weeks ago, that's the whole point of the treatment, but he shot some emboli, developed an arrhythmia and a lung thrombus. With his diabetes he's a management problem for his physician who presently does little but peer at him through thick glasses during the morning rounds.

"How did the night go?" I ask, slumping into his chair.

"Good, good. You're very early, Kata. You anticipate a difficult day?" My name is Katherine. No one but my father ever called me Kata.

"Difficult day, difficult week, difficult six weeks," I say. He does not speak, but raises the shag of his brows so that I see the darkness of his eyes.

"A new rotation of students," I explain, "plus I've inherited two students the faculty expects me to hang."

"Hang?"

"Fail them in the program. Hang's a term faculty uses to mean we compile volumes of anecdotal information. Even with a lawyer, a student shouldn't have a case." I've never before shared confidences with a patient, or anyone but my father. I wonder if that's what I'm looking for, another father. No wonder I'm forty, unattached, in and out of superficial relationships.

"You do not favor a clean slate, free of other's impressions?"

As always, he strikes at the heart of things. "You don't understand," I say. "Six weeks is such a short time. They could slip through my fingers if I'm not forewarned." His look is so benign I stumble on to explain. "It sounds heartless, but getting good grades and being a nice little girl who dreams of being helpful no longer makes a nurse. Technology changed all that. You have to think of the patient, Mr. Karas. If a student can't manage the technical skills, the patient's life is in jeopardy."

I've never called Mr. Karas by his first name, though the rest of the staff do. It's an overt act. I hold him high, or is it away? He's a retired musician, a violinist, who taught orchestra in public schools since immigrating from Czechoslovakia. There is a little accent in his speech, but there are those occasional sentence transpositions that strike me as improvised, poetic.

"This is hard for you, Kata," he says as I leave.

I start this clinical rotation without enthusiasm, with no inclination to seize these first impressions of students. Instead, I find myself resisting, gazing to the back of the room where a bubble of a window gives me snatches of clouds.

There are eight students. Two, according to their former instructors, are unsuitable, but lack the necessary anecdotes to "hang." No wonder I gaze at clouds. I'm expected to scrutinize performance. Those who tremble rate a "double take."

I glance briefly at the eight. Attendance isn't necessary to spot Sara Barr. She's been checked as "inappropriate" in the 'emotional stability' column and "failing" in 'performance skills.'

Ramrod stiff, she sits alone at the back of the conference room, her eyes following me in an unwavering gaze. The other student is Melanie Farnsworth. Her previous instructor has intuitive feelings about Melanie, but few specifics. She caught Melanie in gross violation of asepsis, but the girl claimed to be so upset by the patient's pain she forgot what she was doing. This was excused first semester. The instructor states she feels Melanie will cut corners where she can. There were several other incidents, questionable enough, hardly worse than average. Melanie's dark-haired, pretty, except for a calculated smile when I call her name. I pull myself back from the bubble sky and concentrate on students and their names. Until I know them, I'm dead.

Student assignments are easy this first day. Each has one patient and no responsibility for medications or treatments. They're expected to become knowledgeable enough to take over these functions tomorrow. I wander around answering questions, acting helpful. In reality, I'm watching. Melanie has not taken the restraints off her patient all morning. When questioned she says, "I thought I should leave well enough alone. I was afraid he might grab at his I.V. or tear at his operative site." We discuss restraints and the need to put his arm through range of motion. "OK, I'll do it," she says. Later, she's sitting in his chair, thumbing through a magazine.

I know my irritation is irrational, but I snatch Melanie off to test her on vital signs. With the double stethoscope I listen in as she takes the most difficult heart beats on the unit. She's accurate. Nor does she have any difficulty with blood pressures or a pedal pulse other students have missed. I compliment her and dismiss her to study her patient's chart. She asks if she can take her coffee break now since her patient will probably be needing her later. It's a reasonable request, but I'm querulous. I give permission with a careful smile, which I'm sure she evaluates and finds amusing.

Sara Barr stands outside her patient's room, arms crossed, head high, back straight. Her posturing is regal. Her eyes focus on nothing, as though she guards the palace in some stage performance. Her patient, Eddie, is a nine-year-old with external fixation of tibia and femur. "Need any help?" I ask.

She looks down on me. She is tall. "Not right now, thank you." Her lips are tightly controlled.

"Eddie's finished his bath?"

"He doesn't want one."

As I continue to question, I find Eddie's rejected her. Sara doesn't seem to realize there are other things she can do; study his chart, plan for tomorrow, ask me if she should allow this. I invite her into the conference room. She appears about to break down as I question. I find she has no siblings. "No wonder," I say. "No one can deal with a nine-year-old boy without practice." I take her back to his room to check her on his I.V. change. Instead of moving the equipment, she moves herself. She lowers the tubing by dropping to a crouch, extends it by yanking it violently away from her body and instead of tapping air from the juncture port, she bashes the apparatus against the I.V. pole. She is a flying maze of elbows and action. Impossible to watch. I get Sara and Eddie started on a table game and leave to change her assignment to Mr. Karas.

My other six students are doing well. Three are women with families. They are as one, commuting a half hour from Mt. Horeb, studying together, 'psyching' out instructors, never wasting a second. Maturity counts. They have an emotional niche, a place of security. Hormonal juices no longer drive them crazy. They are able to laugh, to slice out sections of their performance and critique it without apprehension. I envy them.

After clinical, I ask Sara to join me in the conference room to discuss her performance and go over her new assignment. I'm correcting papers when she arrives. Peripherally I can see her standing outside the door, but it annoys me that she neither knocks nor asks permission to come in. I turn to find her rigid, waiting. "Come in, Sara. We're very informal in here. You must feel free to walk in at any time. Nothing I'm doing is more important than a discussion might be." This room doubles as an activity room at certain hours and we sit with the corner of the Ping-Pong table between us.

Sara fidgets with her pen. I make no more attempts to put her at ease. "You probably know I didn't do very well first semester," she begins, her head lowered.

"Do you want to tell me about it, Sara?"

She glances up briefly, then lowers her head again.

"Didn't Miss Bien go over problems in your evaluation?"

Sara makes a face. "What does that mean?" I prod.

"I don't think she thought I did anything right."

"And how did you feel?"

"I really loved taking care of geriatric patients."

"What did you love about it?"

She looks at me as though I might be teasing.

"I'm serious, Sara. What were your greatest satisfactions?"

"Talking to them. They're interesting and they appreciate what you do."

"So you enjoyed their gratitude," I say flatly. Sara looks slapped. "What about the procedures," I continue, "gastric feedings, intravenous feedings, tracheal bronchial toilets. How did you like those?"

"That's not what I call nursing."

"But, you're in a technical program. That's what's expected of you. In this six weeks, expectations go up again."

"They go up too fast," she cries out. "I'm a klutz. I can't go so fast."

"I can't believe you're a klutz. Your file indicates you studied ballet since you were a child. You know well enough that skills take work."

"I can't do it. Not so fast." Her hands fly up as though someone has threatened her with a gun. "I do practice. Mrs. Bell will tell you I'm always in the lab. It's hopeless. Skills exams are just two weeks away." Her voice is shrill, but suddenly it drops and with measured pace she delivers her statement while looking straight into my eyes. "If I don't make it, I'm going right out that window." Her face is flushed, pupils huge and black.

We look at each other a moment. I think of our college's inadequate guidance department, consisting largely of career counseling and financial aid. "Sara, are you telling me that if I find you an unsafe practitioner I must pass you or you're going down seven floors to your death?"

She lowers her head. "Don't lay that on me, Sara," I say quietly. "I'm not qualified to handle it."

I slam into Mr. Kara's room and slump in his chair.

"Our little Sara's a complexity?" he opens, raising a busy brow.

"Our little Sara," I grunt.

"I take it you're not altogether pleased with her."

He laughs at my explosive exhalation. I turn to his eyes, watch him rip through my reserves. I wonder if that's why I love him. Stripped of my façade, he's still my friend.

"I'm preparing Sara's death in this program," I say honestly. "And, she threatens to take her life if I do."

"My poor Kata," he murmurs.

We arrange for silence. I walk to the window to stare at the lake, not wanting to see his thoughts. His response allows me self-pity and tears.

By the fourteenth I have Melanie sewed up. She's appallingly blatant. Each time I confront her, she gives me a 'so-what?' look. She even charts blood pressures she hasn't taken. I become convinced she wants me to shove her out, so I do it with dispatch. Sara's skills do not improve. I can edge her out now or wait for skills exams. I go to lunch, sit alone to fill in my report on Melanie. When I return to the unit, Marge grips my arm. "Mr. Karas must have shot more emboli. Dr. Banks is with him now."

"Twelve fifteen P.M.," the intern announces, turning to me. "They want a post-mortem on Karas, but I don't think there's any rush. It's lunch time." I close the door and sit in the chair beside his bed. His eyes are still open and I look into his non-blinking gaze. "Why did you have to do that?" I accuse.

"I've got a right. Look at my age."

"No, you haven't," I blubber.

"Have a tissue."

"Thanks," I say, whipping out three.

For a time we just look at each other. Finally he says, "I've left you a mess?"

"You know it."

"Listen to me, Kata. Our little Sara feels guilty for her

mother's death and sets up failure for herself."

I stop my snorting and look at him.

"It's true. Instead of letting her punish herself, do it for her." He pauses and raises one shaggy brow. "Understand?"

A great wash of inarticulate understanding floods through me. "Yes," I say.

Two orderlies knock and enter with a stretcher. "They have to have this room ready for an admission. We're supposed to take the body to a holding room."

I stand up, and keeping my back to the orderlies, I take Mr. Karas's hand. "I'll get right on it," I say. "Goodbye, Frank."

Sara's waiting in the hall. "They told me at lunch. I'm sorry," she says. "I know he was your friend."

The energy of my action surprises me as I seize her uniform collar. "Come to the conference room," I growl, tugging her in that direction. I'm aware of lifting heads at the charting desk as I close the door behind us. "Sara, you will be doing skills all afternoon and tomorrow, and tomorrow, and tomorrow. I'm going to work you until you drop."

She stares at me.

"If you don't pass skills exams," I continue, not knowing what I will say next, "you needn't bother jumping out that window; I'll push you."

"Yes," she says, eyes brimming as she smiles.

Perceptions

GRANT HURRIES along the narrow wooded path, blood pressure mounting, Irene close behind. Intellectualizing amounts to nothing. Her mindless habits were there before retirement, his immersion in work protecting him like a membrane. Now they battle like children.

"She never could debate rationally," he mutters. "Her strategy: raise voice, top off statements with some vindictive comment she feels carries the day." Just this morning she'd called him "peevish," following this with such judgmental, self-satisfied little nods, he could only stand there, heart raging against his ribs, measuring her for destruction. That tiny neck, a mere pedicel supporting her nodding head, could be snapped like a twig. It's not the aerobics of the walk that make him pant, it's the woman behind, the woman who follows. He increases his pace, vows to find healthful alternatives before she kills him.

Irene struggles to keep up. He's trying to lose her, knowing full well her fear of this trail, where a young woman was murdered. She runs until he's in sight. "Grant, slow down," she calls. Of course he can't hear, or won't. She runs again, stumbling, crying out before she falls. "Grant," she whimpers, her cheek resting on soft loam. Abandoned, unloved, she struggles to her feet, hurries on, begins to cry. He's never acknowledged her hurts. If she's ill, wanting sympathy, he tells her to see a doctor. Before her breast biopsy he'd said, "Talking about problems before they're confirmed is futile." His exact words. In twenty years she's never forgotten. Tears of self-pity blind her and she stumbles into Grant, who stands frozen in the path. Someone is singing.

A man grips the iron guard rail overlooking the lake. Rocks his body as he sings out over the water. "Harvey's gone," he wails. "We won't see you no more, but I hear your words, I see your smile." His voice rises rich and deep, the sounds of a cantor, the minor key of lament. Grant poises, hesitating as though he might turn back. In a scurrying motion he passes the man, begins mounting the steps to the parking lot. He turns to Irene, rolling his eyes, indicating this is another crazy, impatiently motioning her to follow.

Sounds of mourning, hypnotic in repetition, begin again. Irene advances with caution. As she reaches the man, she stops, touched by the grief in his song. She feels she should reach out to comfort him, and at that moment, he turns. Irene's tears still moisten her face, and that is what he sees. He steps forward. It seems natural that they embrace. Her hands flutter to pat his back. "Thank you," he says, and Irene nods, unable to trust herself to words. 'He has a fine face,' she thinks as she climbs the steps. 'Expressive; a truly fine face and the matte orange of his hair is decorative, quite appropriate for the costume he wears.' Irene climbs with energy, no longer afraid of anything.

Ben's smiling when he hits the club. He sits at the piano, running over the new number, refining, embellishing.

"Hey Ben," Bhomer calls. "Sounds like you got it together."

"Just about," Ben says.

Bhomer thumps two Cokes from the machine and brings them to the piano.

"I had this incredible experience," Ben says, reaching for his Coke. "I went off to the woods, you know, communing with nature, starting the lyrics. I just let go, singing out to the lake and I'm thinking, 'Ben, you got yourself a song'. So sad, breaks me up. Still, I worry. Then I turn and here's this old lady, I mean, she was old, eyes all caved in, but she's got tears running down her face. She's just standin', lookin' at me with all them tears and I know then, I got me a song. Hey, I never expected my muse was gonna be an old white woman, but what the hell. We jus' look at each other and I step up to her and we hug and I say, 'Thank you.' She smiles and kind of nods her head and starts up the steps. I tell you, Bhomer, it's like, hey, beautiful."

Seija

IGNORING THE drone of Reverend Hanson's eulogy, Christine Gjetson eyes his precarious position on the brink of her mother's grave. Those ancient legs, teetering on ragged earth, could drop him in. Hilarity strikes her, and biting her lip, she concentrates on her brother's grief as he grips her hand. There are faces she knows, but she stares past the quick nods of recognition, detaching herself from this town and the curious who look her over. Sliding up the sleeve of her linen coat she uncovers her watch. Six hours before her flight.

Christine looks beyond the open grave to watch her cousin, Peter, rising repeatedly on his toes, soothing his surgeon's legs. His twin, Ralph, catches her eye and winks.

Reverend Hanson's tremolo subsides in quaking prayer before he bends to toss the first fistful of earth. He and her mother had been close. Robert moves to take him in his arms.

Christine feels like a stranger and the knot, tightening her chest, surprises her.

"You gotta be Christine."

Christine turns to the woman she had noticed in a cheap black cocktail dress sequined at the neck and wrists. Now the woman stands before her, a woman in her forties, Christine's age, and she recognizes her at once. "You're Seija."

"Yeah, I didn't think you'd remember me." There is a shy grin that reveals spaces for missing teeth.

"Good to see you again, Seija," Robert says. "You're still in Chicago?"

"I'm still there. I've been married, had a kid, divorced, seems a million years since I left home." There is a forced quality in her speech as though making this contact is painful. "I should a come back here. The best life I had was here."

Christine nods, though her best life was not here. "Were you visiting your family when Mother died?" she asks.

"No, my brother wrote me. I had a come up for her funeral. I couldn't a lived with myself if I didn't at least do that."

Christine stares, incredulous.

"I bet these here are your cousins," Seija says as Ralph and Peter approach.

"Remember Seija Heikintalo?" Christine says, and they smile, nodding vaguely.

"I don't see Donny," Seija says.

"He died last summer," Peter says. "Damaged heart valves."

"I remember him. Older than you guys, but looked younger cuz he was puny."

Peter and Ralph nod.

"You guys still living in Chicago?"

"We left home a long time ago," Ralph says. "Pete's in Boston and I'm near Hartford."

For a few moments they stand awkwardly, avoiding each other's eyes, until Ralph says, "Say Chris, we're thinking of driving out to your mother's house for one last look with Robert. You're coming, aren't you?"

Christine has no desire to see her mother's place. She looks at her watch.

"Oh, come on Chris, it's only ten miles, you have plenty of time."

Once again there is that awkward space until Robert says, "You come too, Seija. Your dad's cabin is just down the beach."

After they've changed and Seija has phoned her brother, they start out in Robert's car. Christine senses the excitement of the twins, who spent their summers with her family until they were well into their teens. Each summer she battled these cousins, subjecting them to her will. Donny had been easy. Though older, he harbored residual fragility from his bout with rheumatic fever. The younger twins formed a formidable unit until Christine became master of divide and conquer. Robert, old enough to ride his bike to town, stayed apart.

It was the summer Christine turned ten that Seija came to the cabin with her father and grown brothers. The Heikintalos lived on a small farm near Bark River, but as soon as the commercial fishing season opened, the father and his sons moved to the beach cabin.

"Is your father still living, Seija?" Robert asks.

"No, Isa died ten years ago, but my brothers are living. Tuelle's fishing in Alaska and Bill lives here. Works at the ore docks. Both bachelors," she laughs and Christine remembers that fragile child as Seija presses her fingers to her lips.

Robert says, "It was always early April when we'd see their trawler anchored in the bay. We marked it like migrating birds."

Christine remembers hearing it chugging out before daylight and sometimes at night. Its deep grunts of fatigue stirred her dreams. "We rarely saw your father or brothers," she says, "but once when I was out fishing with Donny and the twins, the trawler pulled up near our rowboat and your father tossed an enormous fish in the bottom of our boat."

"I remember that," Peter says. "We'd never seen such a fish."

Seija laughs, turns up the cuffs of her dress, hiding the sequins.

"What I remember," Ralph says, "was that Chris got us way out in forbidden waters. Your brothers said they were heading home because of storm warnings. We never could have made it. We would have died in that storm, but your father tied a rope to our bow and pulled us in."

Christine nods, remembering the three amused men, leaning on their elbows, watching the children bob behind. "That was the summer before you came," she says.

"I was ten the winter Mother died," Seija says. "Look, there's French's Island. We're almost there."

The twins lean toward the window and Christine watches the familiar energy she once fought to control. She feels a sudden welling of sadness for Donny. They pass the Halverson farm. "Mrs. Halverson told Mother you were living at the cabin and I was given a sack of cookies and sent off to meet you. I was so mad I sat on the dock and ate most of them because I knew you were older and that you'd be bossy and I was having enough problems with my cousins."

Seija looks surprised. "You were bigger than me."

"I know," Christine says, "when you answered the door the first thing I did was measure you up for size." Robert and the twins laugh. "I handed over the cookies, said I was sorry your mother died, and you just stared at me. Then you said, 'Do you want a cup of coffee?' which thrilled me because I'd never had coffee." Christine closes her eyes remembering Seija standing in the dark frame of the cabin door, the fine white hair floating out in all directions, marking her as a Finn. They had gone into the cabin and Christine watched Seija move around the counter, quick as a bird as she lit the burner, put on water, snatched a plate from the cupboard to lay out two cookies. In her dark jumper and blouse, only her hair held the light.

The cabin had one room. Men's clothing hung from wooden pegs above the hinged cots folded against the wall. Christine asked, "Where do you sleep?" and Seija pointed to the loft where a blanket hung over the rail. She had taken Christine up the ladder; shown her meager possessions. Two brown jumpers hung on pegs and a pair of shoes lay on a shelf. "My school clothes are on the farm," Seija said.

Robert guides the car over familiar ruts as the twins lean out, sniffing cedars, and before Robert stops they are out, galloping to the beach. Robert laughs. "My God, they've just shed twenty years. Come on in. I'll make coffee."

Christine watches as Seija lingers to look at an old family photograph, then walks over to finger the violin that lies on the piano. "Nothing's changed," Seija sighs.

"I'll walk with you if you want to go down to your father's place," Christine says.

Seija shrugs and unerringly selects the right cupboard to collect cups as Robert puts the coffee pot on the table. They sit together and begin to talk and Christine wanders outside. She sees the twins down the beach. Off to the left lies the Heikintalo cabin, still tucked in a heavy shade of spruce.

She had stayed all day, relieved to find Seija more malleable than the cousins, a pleasant surprise not to have every statement challenged by a boy's shrill protest. Seija had shown her the reedy pool where she bathed in sun-warmed waters caught from waves. They waded the tepid water as pollywogs zipped from their shadows.

It was night before they heard the trawler and Seija hurried to the cabin to cut bread, lay out cheese, and crack eggs. She lit the kerosene lamp, for though there was still light on the beach, the cabin was dark. By lamp light the men looked all of one age, Mr. Heikintalo's white hair not that different from his sons.

Christine walks off towards the Heikintalo cabin and suddenly Ralph's heavy arm is across her shoulders. "Kind of sad," he says, "memories getting all shuffled in with the present. I keep hearing Donny's kid-voice and you know, most of the time he's begging us not to ditch him."

Christine slips an arm around Ralph's waist.

"Do you find it a little strange that Seija would make that trip to come to your mother's funeral?"

"I don't know," Christine says. "I never was the daughter Mother wanted. I wouldn't practice, wouldn't dress up, didn't even like dolls. Mother and I had nothing in common. Something happened the first time she saw Seija. Even as a child I recognized the appeal of that skinny little form standing in our door in that awful jumper and her blouse buttoned to the top. She'd wet-combed her hair, flat to her head. Her bangs fell over her eyes, but I could tell it had taken all her courage to visit us, just like now."

They hear Robert calling them for coffee. "Coming, Chris?" Ralph says, dropping his arm.

"In a minute." She watches him jog up the beach. The first hint of fog softens the color of his jacket.

Seija had been at their house all summer. Mother gave her some outgrown clothes and a new lavender dress Grandmother made. Christine refused to try on a dress with ruffles. Seija danced, twisting and turning to catch herself in the mirror. Mother washed and set Seija's hair. When it was dry she combed it out, clapping her hands at the transformation. It was as though she had a doll to dress, but it was more than that.

Christine saw the quick looks of shared secrets and she poured her energy into making life hell for her cousins.

"How would you like to have Seija spend the school year with us?" Mother had said.

"You mean live here?"

"That Chicago aunt is poor, has too many children of her own. A terrible life for Seija. She could have your cousins' room and then, in the summer, she would move back to the cabin."

"No."

"You wouldn't be lonely in the winter."

"I'm not lonely."

"You're alone the minute your cousins leave. It's not right. Think how nice it would be to have a friend. You'd go to school together."

"No. I wouldn't want the kids to think she was my friend."

"Why not? Christine, why not?"

She had wanted to cry, 'Because you love her,' but she narrowed her eyes and said, "Because everyone would know she's a Finn."

"Christine, what have you become?" was all her mother said, but she did not hide a distaste that would separate them.

Christine runs from the memory, hurries to join the others. Robert looks up and pours her coffee.

"She wrote me all the time," Seija says, "even sent clothes, but I never answered. I never answered one of her letters. I was always thinking up things to tell her and never wrote one letter."

"Why not?" Robert asks.

"Seija looks at her hands. "My writing, I never could spell."

"Well," Robert says, "she said you were a very talented child. Said you had perfect pitch."

Seija smiles. "She was teaching me violin, you know. It was a secret." For a moment she seems lost in memory. "My Helme loves music. I'm going to have her start lessons some day."

Christine looks at the cheap black dress and the hands that caress the coffee cup. "Robert, I need to be going. The fog has started."

"You have to take Mother's violin. It's impossible to ship."

Christine stands. "I don't want it. Give it to Seija." She tries to smile at the startled woman, but the words are sour in her mouth. "Mother would like that." She pushes on the screen and walks beneath the cedars. Fog has buried the cabin. It rises from the beach to cover everything.

The Revolutionary

IN THOSE dark days, aware only of broken ribs and other pains, I lay in and out of stupor from the beating. The fact they had not killed me caused no elation, only mild curiosity.

I ate nothing, though I became aware of a bowl being pushed through an opening at the bottom of the door. It was the light, which preceded the scraping of the bowl, that caught my attention. I came to realize my only light source was this one hole, when the flap opened to push in or remove something from my cell. Gradually I began to eat, less for survival than for something to do. The gruel, the very act of eating, was a break in the endless darkness.

Revolutionaries contemplate imprisonment and torture. We are fascinated with tales of survival. I had little concept of time in that place, but gradually became aware of routines. There were the meals. A heavy cart rolling over concrete stopped before each cell. Similar flaps opened as bowls scraped their way into other cells. Booted men who did not speak moved with authority in the corridor. Often there was a strange snuffling around the opening of my cell. Only once did I hear a voice, gentle, soft. I assumed a guard was speaking to his dog. One day, longing for light, I pushed open my door flap and choked on an inward surge of horror. There was no light. The corridor had been lit only for the passing of gruel or similar tasks. No longer detached about imprisonment, I began to fear they knew my identity and were practicing a sophisticated method of torture.

I had read amazing cases of survival in which men wrote whole books in their minds, worked mathematical equations, composed music, but I had no such resources. At the University of La Plata I studied political science, and followed my brother Juan as an activist in the union of Worker's Social Reform. He concentrated on the auto workers of Cordoba, and I in the trading port of La Plata. I was first arrested as an agitator in a meat packing plant. For some unexplainable reason, I was soon released.

News of my brother's murder sent me underground where I was helped to change my identity. Previous to Juan's death I was an idealist, encouraging workers to organize and right their wrongs. In the underground I grew up and became a revolutionary.

Always, always, there was the support of comrades. I did not fear dying. Even after my capture, I made my peace with the world and accepted my end with few regrets. But this prison, this eternity of darkness, moved into the marrow of my being until I feared I would go madly out of control as I had heard about others.

I emptied each bowl of gruel into my toilet, allowing myself only water. When the initial pangs of hunger passed, I gave up water. This lack mercifully clouded my senses so that I experienced neither hunger nor thirst. Finally I lay on my mat beside the little opening. Too weak to empty my bowl into the toilet, I shoved it to one side, overturned it, and placed it for collection. Eventually, hallucinations began.

"Was Hipolito with you?" I asked my brother who squatted beside me on the mat. "No, killed in the Cordoba protest rally."

"Killed? He was only a student. And your friend, Augusto Vandor?"

"Assassinated." Juan's face, unguarded in my presence, contorted out of control. "You cannot expect a union interlocutor to be left standing. They even sullied his name, claiming we killed him for collaboration with them." I saw my brother's open grief turn to rage. "Augusto was true to us."

"It is one of their methods," I murmured. We were silent. "Alfonsin lives?" I ventured.

Juan's face lifted. "A miracle, Arturo," he whispered. "Even the Assembly for Human Rights gains strength. Why they have not come to beat down his door with rifle butts is a miracle." My brother smiled and disappeared.

Giovannina visited to castigate me for our failed relationship. She sat cross-legged in the corner of my cell punctuating each accusation by pounding her tiny fist. I listened, wishing she would leave.

One night, or it may have been day, Mother moved through the wall in her burial gown. In my weakness, I longed for her mother-comfort.

"Arturo, my little son," she said, reaching for me. Like a child I stretched my arms to be taken up. She disappeared and I broke. Dying, sobbing in despair, I determined that all of me would not die in this cell and I pushed my hand and arm through the flap opening.

I heard and felt a snuffling as a snout moved down my arm to my hand. The nose continued over my palm and down the length of my fingers. It was the first living touch I had experienced for months. All my senses awakened. The animal explored each finger, sniffing for long moments. I feared he might stop, and cautiously curled my hand to touch him. As he moved closer I stroked the base of his neck and felt the shag and stiffness of fur, dug into his ruff.

In exhaustion I had to drop my arm, and the dog began to lick as a bitch will do to massage her newborn. Beginning at the base of each finger, she meticulously massaged each finger, my wrist, and arm with concentrated force. Nothing in life had evoked a sweeter sensitivity. I lay absorbed, all my attention focused on the deliberate administrations that sent these sensations, bombarding my brain and effusing my body. When she finished, she settled beside my arm. Placing the flat of my hand on her chest, I felt her beating heart. At peace, I slept.

When I woke, I ate some gruel and lay close to the opening to wait. At last I heard the snuffling and extended my arm. Again I received the ministrations of the dog.

As time moved forward, my inner clock sensed her time of arrival. It was never when the corridor was lighted. She must be shut in. Perhaps to guard.

We had games, a kind of one-armed wrestling. I scratched her, dared to talk and coo through the opening. This continued for months. One day a human hand gripped and released mine and I wept. Sunflower seeds and grapes appeared, buried in my gruel.

When I was moved from my cell, the pain of light made me reel and catch the wall for support. Orders had come from Buenos Aires, where I was to be transferred. Six others shuffled beside me. As we stumbled to the covered truck I scanned the prison yard, waiting for the others to board. Then I saw her. Sitting beside a man, her whole body trembled at attention as she watched me. Like a well-trained hunting animal she waited, under command. I glanced at her master, the supplementer of my diet. Little more than a boy, he barely masked his fear of discovery. I could give no sign, but hold them in memory. It is the source of my strength.

Lake Superior Journal

JAN 4

Peter and I have come to ski. We reached Ontonagon in a series of flights. I thought we might go to one of the lodges in the Porcupine Mountains. We can afford it with my inheritance, but Peter remains frugal and I'm glad. We took a light plane to Hubbell, and in a rented pick-up, traveled northeast. Such signs as Allouez, Bete Grise, and Lac La Belle, pull my attention from this desolate country. "Do you know where we are?" I ask, and Peter, who wants nothing to distract his driving, merely nods. At times we are confronted with great drifts of snow and we pick up speed to hit them solidly. For moments, entombed in darkness, we feel our vehicle shudder before we burst free. These are not cowboy antics. I see Peter grim, determined. For my part there is no fear. Melancholy has held me since my illness.

Three months have elapsed since I've touched my journal, when idiopathic meningitis struck me down. Idiopathic, meaning the doctors were unable to identify the organism, though the symptoms were real enough. I remember none of it, and have been told I was semi-conscious for a week or more. The fever was surprisingly mild. But for attacks of muscle rigidity and a sensitivity to light, there were few other symptoms. I was tube fed. Avertin, given as though I were a tetanus patient, relieved the muscular contractions. The nurses watched closely for signs of muscle spasm, and with the first twitch, gave me more medication. Eventually, I roused from this state to see Peter's face. Even in that somnolent state I saw his exhaustion, in dark hollows that held his eyes.

JAN 5

We have a cabin, fairly isolated from three others that are vacant. We're told they are often occupied during the weekend. We had to leave the truck in town and Mr. Kivisaari's snowmobile pulled us on a great sled that held our supplies. He lives in town during the winter, and was concerned that we understood our stove and that our fire was well-established before he left. Peter seems nervous. He paces. I made pancakes and eggs for supper. When I look out over the vast expanse of ice that is Lake Superior, even ice bound, it seems a sinister presence. We banked the fire for the night and I woke around three to add wood to the coals. All is still.

JAN 6

Nothing could have prepared me for this cold. I gasped as I stepped into it and for a moment had the feeling I might suffocate. One learns to be guarded, to have a mask ready before breathing, or to breathe shallowly. The cold seeps up through your boots, permeates your bones, yet there's a strange exhilaration. I think it's for survival. My melancholy has slipped away. We skied for only an hour today. Peter says I must build up strength. We are eating like wolves.

JAN 7

Another couple arrived before the weekend. Janet and Marv. They're about our age and Janet and I hit it off immediately. She says they're putting off having children. I told her I hoped we'd be able to have them after Peter finishes school. (I didn't mention that he's not really interested in having a family.) They want to ski with us. Marv entertained us with horror stories of this area. People losing their way and freezing. It is an unforgiving environment. Peter seems happier.

JAN 8

It's very pleasant sharing meals with Janet and Marv. Our cabin is larger, so we eat here. Tomorrow we'll ski up the coast, eat lunch in a shelter, and ski home. Mr. Kivisaari said the sauna will be fired up for our return.

JAN 9

It was still early when we turned back, but darkness came on suddenly. I had the feeling we were being followed and looked back to see a dark shape some distance away. It kept closing in, dropping back, melting into the trees. I'm not sure why I didn't mention it to the others, but I was last in line and struggling to keep up. As reluctant as I was to fall behind, I turned frequently to locate its position and try to make it out. When we reached our cabin, I unlatched and kicked off my skis. I turned around for the last time and a feeling of its loneliness struck me, though only shadows moved.

JAN 10

It was a still morning when we skied out on Lake Superior. We had gone less than a mile when a sudden breeze sprang up, followed by violent gusts. Marv was in a panic to get us to shore. Half way in, we heard the ice groan and felt an undulation as though an earthquake were about to buckle all that lay beneath our feet. Peter was well ahead. Exhausted, I would have dropped had it not been for Janet who stopped to urge me on. Safely on shore, we watched, horrorstruck, as the ice broke from the land and floated out steadily as a heavy raft moving out to sea. In minutes it was twenty feet from shore.

"It does that," Marv panted. "Last year two men, cutting ice, were carried out with their truck. The next morning the wind changed and the floe returned to shore. They were able to drive their truck over the ice debris and get on the road."

"The coast guard is always rescuing fishermen from ice floes," Janet said. "Ice fishermen are the maddest of creatures."

JAN 11

Janet and Marv left last night. It's lonely. After watching them, I realize how little Peter and I interact. I was just too tired to notice when I worked to put him through school.

JAN 12

Peter has been restless today. He went off by himself while I was making bread. I didn't go out all day. After supper I noticed the full moon and suggested a little skiing would help us sleep. "Feel free," he said, turning from me. Feeling hurt, unwanted, I dressed quickly. "I won't be long," I said, but he didn't answer. I put on my skis and started along the moon-dazzled trail. I've never seen such stars and at times I'd stop to study the silhouettes of pine. Once again I felt a presence, and though I had no fear, I realized how vulnerable I was if I had an accident. If Peter dropped off to sleep, I might freeze. I started back with caution. There were no lights in our cabin. Placing my skis against our porch, I turned the knob on the door. It was locked. We had never locked the cabin. I knocked, but there was no response. I could see the glow of the banked fire and when I looked in the bedroom, I saw Peter lying on the bed. I hammered on the window, but he didn't move. I called, shouted, fearing he had had a heart attack. Again I tried the door and finally, with the end of my pole, I broke a pane of glass in the door, reached in and turned the key. To my relief, Peter came stumbling from the bedroom.

JAN 13

Peter is revived today. He talked and laughed, seemingly relaxed. It was so windy we did not venture out, but when the sun disappeared there was a great settling. The trees no longer lashed at the sky and the moon rose in magnificence beyond description. Only the lake had motion, and we heard the savage chop of its waves.

After supper Peter suggested we ski by moonlight. We started out around seven and my requests to stop and absorb the beauty were ignored. I fell farther and farther behind. I regretted we would soon be returning to the routine of our work and Peter's long hours at the lab. Peter was well ahead. It was then I felt a threat, far ahead, coming towards me.

Responding intuitively, cautious as an animal, I slipped off my skis and placed them beside me in deep underbrush. I leaned forward and erased my boot prints that stood glaringly distinct in moonlight. Pulling my dark hood around my face I crouched, solid and silent as one of the granite boulders, but so gripped by terror I feared I might cry out and disclose my location. From far off I heard the fierce breathing, then the skis. When Peter passed, I knew I must not reveal myself. He began to call. A kindly voice might have disarmed me, but it was rasping in demand. Once again he passed and I heard his muttered curses. I thought of my strange illness. Dr. Jallings had said, "The lack of fever makes it an enigma. More like a poison than an organism hitting your brain." Was he warning me?

Peter angled off the main path on the trail to the shelter. I put on my skis. It was seven miles to town. I had a head start. I arrived at the Kivisaari's in a state of exhaustion. They have taken me in. Several men have gone off to look for Peter, but a storm came up and they had to call it off.

JAN 14

They found Peter's frozen body before noon, he had fallen and broken his leg. I am sick with guilt and allow the kindly Mrs. Kivisaari to manage me. She has put me in to bed, but I lie awake knowing I am responsible for Peter's death. I imagined his frantic search as sinister. My brain, sick from the illness, has twisted all reality. The phantom is proof enough that my mind is sick.

JAN 15

Mr. Kivisaari took me to our cabin. I packed and placed Peter's belongings in his duffel with great sadness, but when I opened his wallet for traveler's checks I found a note I had written before Mother's death. I'd been visiting Mother for three days. It was painful to be separated from Peter and I left her, earlier than planned, to hurry home. I found our apartment empty and called the organic chemistry laboratory, but Peter hadn't been in. Frustrated, nearly in tears, I went to the kitchen to make coffee. Every dish in the house was dirty and stacked in the sink. At that point I did cry and wrote, "Peter, at times like these, life doesn't seem worth living." Placing it under the light by the sink, I went to bed. Peter had saved it.

Settling In

"IF YOU want to see me alive you'd better get over here," my father-in-law threatens.

"We'll come as soon as John gets home," I say.

My husband's siblings respond individually to calls from the nursing home. John scolds, Frank laughs, Sonny makes promises, and Betty cries, but they all get there.

We find Dad waiting for us in the reception room, his small bag packed. "We're going to Manitowoc to see Florence," he announces. "They're not treating her right in that new housing project. Someone's got to raise hell."

"Dad," my husband says, "it took me six months to get her in that place. You know Florence."

"I know my sister," Dad shouts, his face florid as a raging child. "Five feet tall. What can she do? She's being absurd, I tell you. I haven't slept or eaten since I called her."

John looks at me and sighs. "I could correct papers on the drive up," I say.

John scowls and turns to Dad. "What about signing you out for an overnight? Doesn't the doctor have to approve or something?"

We're near the nurse's station. They pretend not to hear, but I read their faces. 'Take him. Give us a break.'

"OK," John says, "but next time, call someone else. I sit the next three out."

We stop for dinner along the way. John's preference would have been bacon and eggs, but I hear Dad's directions. As I splash at papers in the back seat, he turns around to watch me. "Hungry? You're going to love this place."

He's expansive in the restaurant, ordering expensively, sending back a soup that's not boiling. "Did I tell you Alta Seymore died?" he begins.

"No," John says. "I didn't know you knew her."

"She was at the home at the last," Dad says. "I got to know her very well."

John risks a look at me. The Seymores are society. It's hard to picture Alta Seymore and Dad exchanging two words.

"That poor woman was never happy," Dad says. "Clinton was a self-absorbed man."

'And you aren't?' I think. I've never heard Dad's children speak of him without the sting of anger.

"She said to me, 'if only we'd met long ago.'"

"That's nice," John says, chewing his way through a hard roll.

Dad sips his coffee. "After Alta was laid out, her friends had to wait to see her because the family was not satisfied. A devoted family. They took her wig home and washed it, and put a lavender hanky in her hand. I, myself, saw them patting on more rouge."

"Is everything all right?" our waitress asks.

"Just about perfect, darlin'," Dad says, "if you warm up this coffee." I can see the younger man in the smile he gives her. When we go, he insists John leave an outrageous tip.

Florence has grown cute in old age though her eyes snap, dissatisfied as ever. Round, all in pink, she throws herself into John's arms, gives her brother a peck, and looks at me as always, as though she can't quite place me. "It's a terrible place," she confides. John looks around. I can see he's pleased with the neat little apartment. "This is much nicer than the dump you were in," he says.

"I don't like the people," Florence says. "They're old and have nothing to do but gossip."

"Isn't Margaret Purty here? You've known her a long time."

Florence fixes John with a look. "I've hated her since we were in high school."

There's a knock. "Get that, Johnny," Florence says. Frank and Sonny enter. The brothers are astonished to see each other.

"When there's a family crisis we pull together," Dad bellows, shaking hands with his sons. Sonny looks around smiling, confused. He's twenty years younger than his siblings. Though forty, bald, and chubby, he's the baby and they keep him there. A barely perceptible smile twists Frank's lips. "Where's Betty?" he asks.

"She'll be here," Dad says. "She's over a hundred miles farther than Madison." We all know that. I'm shocked. Betty hasn't been well since her husband's death.

"So what's the crisis?" Frank asks.

"I think we'll wait until Betty's here," Dad says. "Florence, aren't you going to give us coffee?"

"Always running the show. That's you, Ross. I can serve coffee without your direction, thank you." She hustles to the kitchen and I follow, uneasy with the way things might go.

Cookies have been set out and there are sandwiches in the refrigerator. "How nice," I say. "I love your apartment, Florence, especially the way you've decorated."

She's pleased and begins to show it off, taking me to her bedroom, cozy with lamps and a chair for reading. "Take a look at this closet," she says, opening the door to a walk-in.

"I'm jealous," I say and she winks.

The coffee and food have just been set out when Betty arrives. Exhausted, unresisting as a rag doll, she allows Dad to fold her in his arms. "Thank you, darlin' girl. You are a loyal child." She glances around at the assemblage, smiles wanly at me. John gives her his chair and sits on the floor.

Frank leans toward his father. "So tell us," he says, letting his cynical smile escape its usual confines, "what crisis demands this pilgrimage to Manitowoc?"

"I think," Dad says, edgy for the first time, "we'll eat what Florence has prepared. I don't want anything unpleasant to spoil this beautiful spread."

Florence sits on the couch and begins to pour coffee. "Pass the plates and food, Sonny." The door opens and Margaret Purty enters and takes Sonny's place. She's wearing a large black wig that shoots straight up from her narrow forehead. "You all know Margaret," Florence says. Margaret gives us an appraising look. "The whole tribe," she comments.

"I knew your older sister," Dad begins.

"Well, she isn't dead yet," Margaret says. "I hope to live to see her eat humble pie."

Frank and Florence laugh.

"Someone's moving into Essie's old apartment across from you," Margaret says. "They're putting his stuff in now."

"His stuff?" Florence says.

Margaret snickers.

"Essie lived there," Florence explains. "Died of a broken heart. Her son brought her here. He told her he was taking her out to dinner and she dressed in her best, a powder blue suit. Remember how nice she looked, Margaret?"

Margaret makes no secret of her wig, but pushes it back an inch to scratch. "He just dumped her and left. She talked to us a lot. Said her children would hang up whenever she called. We tried to make her think her kids just wanted her to settle in."

"Nothing wrong with her head when she came," Florence says, "but after a few months she started making phone calls to her husband to come and get her. She'd told me, herself, he was long-dead. Later, she started to worry about her children playing in the street or she'd be thinking she had to do something like buying them shoes."

"Then she went into phase three," Margaret says. "That's what the nurses called it. She started crying for her mother and you'd swear there was a little girl in her apartment."

"How terrible," Betty says, sinking back in her chair.

"Kids," Florence snorts. "Frankie and I are the smart ones." She leans to ruffle Frank's remaining strands of hair. "We never had kids."

There is a rumbling in the hall. "Open the door, Sonny," Florence says. He opens the door and we see two men rolling a large T.V. into the apartment across the hall. A thin, forlorn man watches.

"Yoo-hoo neighbor," Florence calls. "Don't be a stranger." The man moves hesitantly to her door and smiles.

"Come in, come in," Dad trumpets. "I want to look over this fellow who's going to live across the hall from my sister." Florence giggles and the new man enters. The brothers rise to shake his hand. Frank gives up his seat.

Karl Ketterling is from Two Rivers. I listen as connections are made, mutual acquaintances revealed. Except for color, Margaret Purdy and Florence wear identical wigs. With my eyes half-closed, Florence becomes Zsa Zsa Gabor. Dad sparkles in his suit. Faded with fatigue, the rest of us wait. The new man is smiling at Florence. "What a wonderful family," he says.

Kata

KATA, PILLOWED high in her bed, eyes closed, separates thick chestnut strands of her hair with white fingers before each savage yank of the comb. I lie on my cot watching my sister.

She's grown weaker, and lately my parents openly discuss this with my older sisters. I'm no longer excluded from their whispers and I hover in the grip of foreboding.

Kata opens her eyes, glares across the room into some distant space. "What time did they leave?"

"Right after breakfast," I say. "Do you want your breakfast now?"

"So, you got out of Auntie's funeral? You have to tend me. My nine-year-old nursie." Kata's voice punctuates in short sharp stabs.

I rub my face across my blanket's rough wool, comforted by familiar irritation that burns my cheek. "I'll get your breakfast."

"I don't want it."

"But, Sam's coming. Don't you want to finish eating before he gets here?"

"I just want to get my damned hair combed. Just want my damned hair to look nice." Her voice cracks and I'm afraid she'll cry.

"I'll comb it," I say. "Eat first and then I'll comb it." She flings the comb to the floor and turns her face to me.

In the kitchen I complete her tray with a slice of white toast and jelly and the oatmeal she likes. I know she won't drink the milk, so I put it in the red and silver goblet Mother used to tempt us children when we were sick.

Mother said Kata put on a brave front, having to miss her own graduation. Afterwards, when her boyfriend, Sam, and a load of their friends, still in caps and gowns, came out with her diploma, they had a party and plunked a mortarboard on her bouncing curls. It was a wonderful party. She laughed and Sam kissed her right in front of everyone, and mother who always worried that excitement was not good for Kata's heart, didn't say a word.

Almost a year and her friends have gone off. Only Sam comes, and that's just once a week when he's home from college. They will be married as soon as she's better, but now we know, even Kata must suspect, that she will never be better.

Someone always sleeps on the cot in her room. At first we took turns, but I really wanted to be with her, so we quit rotating. Kata puts on a bright face for everyone, but I see the changes. One night she said, "Go to your own room awhile. I'm going to rant and rave and probably curse and I can't do it with you here."

"Why not?" I said, "I know curse words."

"Not as many," Kata said, "I'm nine years older. Now get. I want to be alone."

I got off my squeaky cot and bedded down in the living room. After that, I pretended to be sleeping whenever I heard the snap of her lamp or the first snuffling of tears. I even became used to the anger and paid no attention. Kata might announce, "I'm going into a full scale snit. You might like to take your homework to the kitchen." Afterwards, we graded her anger from petulance to rage and sometimes argued over the degree.

She hates being dependent. From the beginning she wouldn't

have anything to do with a bedside commode. Dr. Bantish didn't like that, but said he didn't have the energy to fight such a strong-willed girl. Lately she's been taking walks around the house at night. Says it's to build up her strength. I'm the only one who knows, and I watch her struggle and wonder if I should tell.

"That's it, Nursie," Kata says, laying down her spoon.

I take the tray to the kitchen, return to pick up the comb, and climb on her bed. On my knee I begin to comb the great bunches of hair. Gramma says Kata's hair sucks her strength and should be cut, but Kata won't have it.

I've just finished combing when we hear Sam's truck begin its long struggle up the first grade past the Dickenson farm. Kata heads for the bathroom to put on make up. "Get my yellow blouse, will you?"

I make the bed, smooth a plaid coverlet over it and race to the closet to dig out her new yellow blouse. Normally I would not be helping her dress, but Sam's truck has begun its coughing and we know it's close to the upper grade of our hill. I see her naked, the thrust of bony hips, ribs, vertebrae like a length of beads down her back.

"You look pretty," I say once she's dressed. Kata glances in the mirror. "Think so?" She's breathless. I can see the pallor around her mouth and the beginning of faint blue tips on her fingers. Determinedly, she walks to the front room and sits on the couch.

I watch Sam step from his truck. He glances at the house before picking up the book that lies on the truck seat. The morning sun strikes his glasses. I can't interpret his wince.

I swing open the front door when Sam reaches the step. "Where is everyone?" he says.

"Auntie's funeral."

Sam ruffles my hair with his free hand and sees Kata on the couch. "What's this? Is this allowed?"

Kata laughs. "I'm getting strong. I walk around every night. Tell him, Emi."

"It's true," I say. "It's still a secret. Want coffee?"

"Course he does," Kata says, her face flushed with excitement.

I go to the kitchen, pour the coffee, and butter two of the morning biscuits for him.

"You spoil me," he says as I place the plate on a side table.

"She's in love with you," Kata says.

"I am not," I screech, but I'm pleased to have him know and dash to my room upstairs.

One of my sisters said Sam doesn't have sex appeal. That night I asked Kata about it and she said, "Now listen, Emi, I'm going to tell you something important. Sex appeal's in the mind and it starts this chemical reaction. Actually, women are looking for a mate who will give them babies and protect them. Long ago women had to have someone who could beat off the enemy and run down animals, but today we don't need a big ape with a gun on his hip. Our stupid sisters are confused, probably because of the movies, just look at the guys they date." She did an imitation of Shawn Bell and we both collapsed in giggles.

"Does Sam have sex appeal?" I asked.

"Sure, but like I said, it's in the mind. Sam's smart and one of the first things that attracted me to him was the way he was taking notes in the library. I even liked his glasses."

I'm in charge of lunch. I lie on my bed and go over the menu, but Kata and I talked late last night and I fall asleep.

"Emi, Emi," Sam calls from the foot of the stairs. "Come down and hear what your crazy sister is saying."

Kata is standing by the couch. "I want to," she says. "This is my only chance and I'm going to do it."

Sam's pacing, breathing like he's been in a race. "She wants to ride the bike down the hill."

"It wouldn't take any effort," Kata cries. "It's all down hill. You follow me and after I've done it, you can throw the bike in the truck and bring me home. I want to do it, Sam." Kata holds out her arms. "I want to feel the movement and the wind. I want to feel alive."

"But what if you fall?"

"If," Kata snorts, "but ok, if I fall I get skinned up. So what? It's not going to hurt my heart. Don't worry so much. I won't go on the steep grade past Dickenson's."

Sam is wringing his hands and turns to me, but I can see Kata's mood.

"She'll do it, anyways," I say. "She'll just do it at night and I'll have to pull her back on the wagon."

"Sit down, sit down everyone," Sam says, patting the air with both hands. We sit, we argue and it's decided that after lunch, after her nap, Kata will ride the bike down the hill. She throws her arms around Sam and kisses him.

What she's about to do detracts from the lunch I've prepared and it makes me a little mad because Sam hardly notices his food. "Do you think she's strong enough?" he asks after Kata has gone to bed.

"The brakes are good," I say, not really caring. "I don't think she'll have any trouble with the brakes." He looks relieved and takes another helping of meat balls. "I don't know about her balance," I continue. "She holds on to furniture when she's walking around the house."

"Oh God," Sam moans, laying down his fork. "What can we do?"

"I don't think we can do anything. Do you want more milk?"

"No, thanks. If only your folks would come home early."

"What book did you bring?" I ask.

"*Anna Karenina*. Did she finish *Penguin Island?*"

"Yes, we read it and loved it when the near-sighted missionary started preaching to the penguins, and especially when he baptized them. Kata says I understand satire as well as anyone."

Sam nods his head.

Kata steps from the porch when Sam wheels the bike from the garage. The wind's strong enough to catch her hair and lift it from her back. She smiles and takes quick steps.

"Now wait," Sam directs. "I want to have the truck started, ready to go, before you get on. I want to hold the bike and get you started."

Kata leans over to kiss him on the cheek. Her face is flushed and she's so beautiful I can only stare at her.

"Hold the bike, Emi," Sam says.

When the truck is started, perking to Sam's satisfaction, he swings down and holds the bike as she mounts. "Please, Kata, let's junk this plan."

"No," she says, excitement flooding her face.

Sam supports the bike for a few feet. "Let me go, let me go!" Kata cries. Sam races to the truck.

We follow and he keeps enough distance to stop in case she falls. "She's letting it go. She's not braking at all," Sam says. "Yell at her to brake." He pulls the truck beside the speeding bike. "Brake, brake," I cry. Kata's face is transfixed in ecstasy. She squints her eyes against the wind.

"Get ahead of her and make her brake," I shout and Sam speeds ahead. On the curve Kata fools us. As she careens around the truck, we hear her shrieks of laughter as she passes. All of Kata comes to me: her pranks, our night talks, her wild love of things.

"She's going too fast," I cry. "She'll never be able to stop before Dickenson's hill."

"Emi," Sam shouts. "Slide over here and take the wheel. I'm going to pass her and jump out. Can you steer it to the side and stop?"

"Yes," I screech.

We speed up and pass and I grab the wheel as he opens the door. Before I've stopped the truck, I'm sobbing The bike lies between us, the front wheel spinning. Sam holds Kata in his arms. Blubbering, I stumble to them as they sway together shimmering against the light. Sam pulls me in and rocks us as we mourn the last of Kata's laughter.

Getting On With It

"HELLO," I call, pushing my voice ahead to shield me as I enter. She does not answer and I step into her bedroom where the night light outlines the bald head. Her face is lost in darkness and I wait, hoping she is dead.

"I need it now!" she hurls at me, eyes squeezed shut. Her voice can still project, enunciation sharp, crisp.

"Is the pain bad?" I ask stupidly. She doesn't bother to answer. I go to the bathroom to prepare the Demerol. "You want the whole thing?" Sometimes she will take only half and I squirt the rest down the drain. When she does not answer I take it all to her.

Elizabeth can no longer turn herself and I roll her as gently as I can. I have to switch on the overhead light to be certain where to give it. She's so thin. I press to find the depth of tissue, a bit of muscle for the injection.

"Just give it!" her voice crescendos, petulant. She becomes quiet, waiting for the effect. I move to a chair by the lamp and pull out lecture notes. I am falling behind in my work. There's trouble at home. I must learn to compartmentalize, to seize the moment for what it can mean, like now. There should be thirty minutes. I begin to read.

"You shouldn't read in that light." I look up at her, high above me in the rental hospital bed, a *Star Trek* princess with enormous eyes in the shadowy hollows of cheek bones. I resist telling her she's beautiful. She would hoot at that.

"Did you accomplish much?" she asks.

"Enough," I lie. I want to tell her about the problems at home. Things John has said. "Ready to work?" I ask.

Elizabeth laughs as I pull out the tape recorder and spiral notebook. Her laugh hasn't changed. I recall first hearing it sail from their back porch, through trees and down the gully and up to where we lounged in summer darkness, swatting mosquitoes. Twelve years! John had the monocular on them as they moved in. "They have a little girl. Looks about Margie's age."

My intentions had been good. Take cookies, introduce myself, but Mother was sick and juggling work and the family was more than enough. I think Elizabeth always resented us for not welcoming them. 'When the Mattsons moved into the neighborhood,' Elizabeth said, 'they were so hungry for friendship I thought Joyce would cry when I took over a cake.' She and Joyce became good friends. I met Joyce for the first time at PTA.

Our girls played together. Margie and Jessica, always together, conniving, hatching plots in the tree house between our yards. Elizabeth didn't always approve of me and came on strong, forceful as her voice. On Saturdays I often heard Elizabeth and Joyce visiting on the screened porch.

"You're going to have to help me with this next memoir. Remember when Jessica and Margie ran away, took the rowboat, thought they would eventually get to the ocean?" She laughs, "Of course those two would have made it."

I had almost forgotten. "They even took their cats. Hadn't they been reading *Paddle To The Sea*?"

"Something like that. I've been thinking and jotting down

details all day. Can you remember anything more?"

I turn to her notebook, scan her spidery notes, absorbed now. Our weekly project is turning out nicely. She works on a memory, we hash it out, and she records. I take it home to type. I am saving the tapes for her family. Sometimes I cry when her longing to be part of them peeks through.

I pause to look at the moon between our two back yards. Jessica called, asking me to "baby sit" her mother. I wonder if Elizabeth could have heard.

Except for our memoir sessions, I only go over when no one else is home. Allan might have a meeting twice a week, but one of the kids is usually there. Jessica sounded tightly controlled, as though they have been fighting. Her voice's like Elizabeth's, though untrained. I amble up their hill and enter through the screened porch. The moon floods everything. Jessica darts into the bathroom as I enter Elizabeth's room.

My daughter told me Jessica has been to Planned Parenthood for a diaphragm. It was not told as a confidence, but flung at my head. They are fifteen! At fifteen, I discovered Lawrence Olivier in *Wuthering Heights* and saw it four times.

"Bye, Mom." Jessica stands at her mother's door. I see the stubbornness of her lower lip. They have been fighting. Jessica hesitates a moment, then comes forward to give her mother a peck on the cheek. I suppose she is still too overwrought to thank me for coming. We hear a car in the drive and she flounces out in her peasant skirt, hair flowing.

Elizabeth gives a hopeless, exasperated sigh. "Jessica thinks she has to go out because her boyfriend feels uncomfortable here." Her voice is matter-of-fact, brisk. "It was nice of you to come,

Ruth. Allan shouldn't be late. Did this interrupt anything?"

"No."

"You don't have your books."

"End of the week. Time to relax."

"Let's have a drink." Her tone is conspiratorial. I've never seen her like this.

She insists on their best glasses, though she must sip with a straw. We drink several and hazily I consider her body weight and the combination of Demerol and alcohol.

"Lie down on Allan's bed. That's a fresh pillow on the other side." She seems to want this, and I lie with my head at the foot of the double bed so we can face each other. I've kicked off my shoes and feel terribly comfortable, like falling asleep. From where I lie, only her eyes seem significant. Shadowed with endless dark spaces behind them, they sometimes catch the light from the hall. They are always on me. Way up above the ridge of her bed she looks down on me as I struggle against sleep.

"Tonight is a kind of anniversary for me," she says. "In a way it is for you, too." She seems to be trying to lift her glass for a toast, but can't quite manage it. I close my eyes, not wanting to watch. "Ten years since my first surgery. Remember? You stayed with me that first night."

"And you didn't even need me," I laughed, recalling her gutsiness.

"It was Allan's idea. He didn't want me to be alone."

I think, as I had then, 'so why didn't Allan stay?' "Ten years," I say.

"Remember, Allan insisted the kids see it as soon as the dressings were off? He didn't want any misconceptions." She laughs and I open my eyes. All I can see are black spaces where her eyes are watching. "As though any of us had any real conception. That revelation comes in stages. A curtain's drawn back, you see what's ahead, but only as far as the next curtain. They go on and on and you think this has got to be the end of it, but no, there is still another horror behind the next one. Did you know I finally went into therapy?"

"No, I didn't know."

"Of course not." Her voice is a whip. "You and I were never close."

"Whatever became of Joyce?" I ask, implying that I don't see her good friend spending evenings with her.

"You knew they moved?"

"That much I've heard."

"They divorced soon afterwards. She has the kids."

"She was so beautiful," I say, remembering Joyce in a peach sweat-shirt at some neighborhood function, her face peach, her hair not far from that color. She moved like a dancer. "What happened?"

"He was having an affair with Libby."

"Libby!" I almost sit up.

"You really don't know what goes on in the neighborhood, do you?"

"I work," I say.

Elizabeth catches the self-pity and it makes her smile. "It wasn't the affair that bothered Joyce, she had known that for years." Elizabeth pauses, watching me, pacing herself. "But, when Walter hung Libby's drapes, it was too much."

I explode and Elizabeth moves her head a little, catching the light. I can see her pleasure in my response. "Walter wouldn't even empty the garbage for Joyce," she says.

"But how could it happen with their houses just across the

road from each other, their kids in and out?"

"That affair took place on Joyce's super market day."

This time we both laugh. I picture Walter lumbering across as soon as Joyce roars away in her VW. I wipe my tears. "Skinny Libby," I say, "so determined, so grim. I can't imagine Libby and Walter---."

"In bed? I can. She would be in charge and give all the directions. That's what Walter's always needed. 'Don't take anything but your pants off, Walter, there isn't time.'"

I roll on my back helpless with laughter.

"Libby's just like his mother. Have you met his mother?"

"No."

"I tell you, we're programmed right from the start. There's no escape. Even cancer. Look at my poor sister and two cousins, Aunt Harriet, Grandmother Bender."

"Your mother's hearty."

"Oh well, Mother. She'll never die of anything. She's had it all removed."

Elizabeth seems to be trying to sustain our tipsy euphoria —or is she bringing up cancer for new direction? I fidget with my sweater, buttoning up, waiting for her lead.

"Ten years," she says so softly I strain to listen. "Of course, Dr. Markum is so straightforward. When he said that with chemotherapy I might have ten years, it seemed a long way off. Besides, there would certainly be a break-through in the cancer world. Naturally there was no mention that if cancer didn't kill me, chemotherapy would. He's a great believer in aggressive therapy," Elizabeth speaks in her splitting Bette Davis voice. "After all, that's what his research grant is all about."

I hear a car in the drive and move to the window. "Allan's home."

"Saved by the bell," she says.

I look at her, but her eyes are shut. I put her wig in place. "Is there something I can do before I go?"

"No." She makes a face as she adjusts the wig.

In a few moments we hear Allan calling cheerily. "Hello, hello, anybody home?"

"My god," she says, her eyes still shut.

I move through the bare trees, scuffing the leaves at the bottom of the gully before climbing the hill to Elizabeth's house.

"I can smell the cold on you," she says reaching to touch my coat. "How was your week?"

I shrug. "Wish I had something exciting to tell you. Classes are OK. You have a new lamp. I like it." The new fixture casts a soft glow over everything. There are no sharp shadows.

She pulls at her wig. "Damned itchy thing. Put it on the dresser."

We have completed six stories and tapes and are pleased with our progress. This is still a secret from her family. Elizabeth became anxious that something might happen to the tapes and I had duplicates made. She's afraid Allan will think they might depress Jessica, so I keep copies in my file to give Jessica when she's older. "Older" has not been defined.

We work steadily for an hour, and Elizabeth calls for a break. "I need a shot, too." I go to prepare it. "I want it all," she calls from the bedroom.

In the kitchen I pour out juice and stare at the ladyfinger she's offered me. Finally I plunk it on the tray and go into her bedroom. We're sipping juice when Elizabeth says, "You're gaining weight."

"I wouldn't be eating this if you hadn't offered it to me," I grumble.

"My fault," she snaps. By the new light I see a fleeting glint of hatred.

"I always gain twelve pounds in the fall and keep it on all winter. I think I've the genes of a squirrel to build up winter padding."

"You would like my sister Peg, except she never takes it off. The last time I visited her, I was appalled. She ate everything in sight. I mean that. She cleaned up everything on the table except the butter and when we went to her studio, she lay on the floor. Peg doesn't have a large studio, but she filled the room. This huge mound on the floor. It was alarming. I've been trying to get her to go to my shrink."

"You have one you like?"

"You never like your shrink. It's love-hate. In my situation it's a relief to talk to someone who doesn't tippy-toe around being so god-damned cheerful."

I know what she means and I nod, slipping my eyes up to meet hers.

"Which reminds me, I want you to give Allan a call. He's in a meeting. Tell him to bring home some milk."

"Sure."

"Just press dial 3. It's programmed for his office."

I put through the call, uneasy with her intensity. I wonder how she can use the milk situation to check on him. The refrigerator's bulging with milk cartons.

"No answer?" she asks.

"Line's busy," I lie, but she's not taken in. "I'll try again."

The pain is constant now. We have had to abandon our project. Sometimes I see the hatred beneath her heavy lids. Why not, with my trivia talk, my health? I wish I could be deeper for her but I can only go where she takes me. When the pain's dimmed, she rambles and I trudge behind. "I've endured everything," she says, "but I can not endure the pain. I can not get out of bed to that bathroom where I could end this." I'm certain she knows I'm afraid she'll ask me to do what I will not do. I feel I've failed her. She has me dial Joyce and insists I sit in her room while they talk. There's no mention of pain. She tells Joyce I am gaining weight and later tells me some of the things Joyce says about me. She screams when I give her an injection, claiming I don't know what I'm doing. Later she says, "It's the pain that makes me lash out. It's just that you were here."

My husband looks up when I come in. He doesn't greet me. Lately he's become more critical of the time I spend with Elizabeth. "Let them hire someone. They have a nurse all week. Let them get one when they go out."

"Allan offered to pay me."

"He knew you wouldn't take it."

"She wants me."

John laughs. "Great. Big ego trip for you."

"My god, she dying."

"For how long? How long has she been dying?"

We glare at each other and I wish him an hour of her pain. I pick up my uncorrected papers and go to my desk. Tonight she spoke of her shrink helping them with the grief process, years ago. I strained to hear her soft murmuring. "We went through it together, the boys crying, Jessica clutching. I remember Allan suddenly grabbing me. We both cried. It was really a beautiful time." Her lids lowered to the memory. When they lifted, her voice regained its resonance. "They worked it through, said their good-byes, but I'm still here." Looking at me, she said, "Now they wish I would get on with it."

"No!" I cried, certain it was true.

I hear John in the hall. "Coming to bed?"

"In a minute."

He pushes back my door. We look at each other across that space. "You're getting involved," he accuses.

"Up to my ears," I say, feeling nothing for him. When he leaves I turn out the lights and move to the window. I can see Allan's silhouette as he reads in their living room. In the bedroom, Elizabeth's faint light reflects on winter trees.

Helmut

ELLEN WATCHES his walk to the barn, his progression deliberate, oblivious to the young dog's whirls and skids for attention.

She can see his aging better from a distance. At meals, his hands, his chewing, his silences, are not that changed. He stops by the barn, staring down, and she wonders if he's missing his son, but it's the belt on the binder he stoops to examine.

It is she who misses Dan, though it was her urging that pushed him to leave. She wonders if she did the right thing, wonders about Sullivan's boy, who didn't leave.

Ellen turns to the mantel where Dan's graduation smile rushes out to her. His picture's flanked by sisters, both mothers now, with lives of their own. Dan would have stayed for her, but she could not have him sour to the sarcasm of his father, for that was how they fought once Dan was grown. Ellen watched the beginnings, not yet shaped. In time he'd be molded to his father's form, his growing defiance invading his bearing as a mineral adds to bone.

Ellen glances at the mantel clock and turns to her kitchen to ladle soup, slice bread, and set Helmut's pie on the sideboard. She senses him plodding towards the back entry, hears him dropping his Wellingtons before washing up.

"Your pup reminds me of Ginger," she says as he sits at the table. "Maybe that old dog reincarnated herself to be near you."

"This one will never be Ginger," he says, slapping butter on the bread he's palmed.

"Give her time, Helmut. How much did you know at six months?"

He does not answer, but dips his head to the soup.

Suffocated, she wonders why she continues to try with this man. She glances at his lowered head, at the great shock of wild hair that has followed the pull of his woolen cap. It was just this wildness, this silence, that attracted her. She had been so aware of him watching as she danced at her cousin's wedding. He didn't dance, not a man like Helmut, but stood apart, eyes hidden by depths of brow and cheekbones. Only a blackness followed her as she consciously laughed, knowing he watched. Later they strolled her uncle's long side porch where he claimed her like some rough Heathcliff.

Everyone objected. "He's a loner," her mother cried. "He'll drag you off to some isolated farm where you'll work from morning to exhaustion. You're a town girl, Ellen. You just don't realize. If only your father were alive."

"Course he picked her," she overheard her uncle say. "All that dancing, all that energy. He picked her like he would his cattle."

"Ready for pie?" she asks and the great head turns to the sideboard. She hands it to him and watches his ritualistic attack, unchanged. He will leave the butt of the crust, though she's known for her crusts.

She had surprised herself with the ease of slipping into farm life, enjoying her hens and kitchen garden, even field work. Beds of flowers and young fruit trees flourished from that first summer and by the time her home was cozy and bright, the children began.

They both hear it, the mail truck's lurching departure. "Mail," Helmut announces and she rises to get it.

She's in no hurry to reach the mailbox. "It was the miracle of children that made life dear. I made him up," she says, stopping. "I had to believe in my idea of him." Ellen looks down at the pup's eager attention. "He'll starve you, too," she says, bending to stroke the smooth head.

A letter, in unfamiliar rounded script, is addressed to her. The return address is Gladstone. "Who on earth?" All relatives have died or left Gladstone long ago. There is such a thumping of her heart, she slips the letter in her apron and carries the remaining stack to lay before Helmut. She clears dishes, intermittently fingering the pocketed letter. When Helmut stands to leave, she asks, "Why don't you take the pup with you? She's lonely when you're gone."

He turns a confused face to her. He has heard, but has not processed her question and must think back on the words. "She's a nuisance," he says, pulling on his town jacket.

After he starts the truck Ellen watches him drive to the road, the dog trailing. She opens the door and calls her back. Overjoyed, the pup comes back full tilt and Ellen can not close her out. "You'll have to stay in the kitchen. Look at those dirty paws. Big paws. You're going to be a big dog." The pup, delighted to hear this, gallops around the table in skids. Ellen sits at the table and pulls out her letter. "Kermit Bender? Why in the world is Kermit Bender writing to me?" She reads it aloud as she reads everything, to hear a voice.

Dear Ellen,

Several months ago I was visiting my cousin in Walhalla, North Dakota, who promised me fishing on the Pembina. Anyways, while waiting, drinking coffee and looking over his newspaper, my eye caught an ad for the sale of five Holsteins by a Helmut Luoto who lives near Leroy. Don't ask me how I remember you married a Finn named Luoto, but seeing it in print seemed right, even the first name. So, I cut out the ad intending to give you a call just for the fun of saying 'hello' and 'guess who,' but you know how it goes. One thing led to another and the fishing was good and before I knew it I was back in Michigan. Yesterday I came across the ad tucked in my shirt and said to myself, 'Write her a letter.' So here I am, Ellen...the guy you creamed with a wooden spoon in kindergarten. I could go on, but more important, what are you up to? Grandmother yet? We have six. All in the Escanaba-Gladstone area. I've retired from Dad's hardware and am living the good life which, as you know, can only be on Lake Michigan shores or in a boat. So...how about it? I'm not going to tell you everything in one letter, but promise to reveal more about Gladstone people and old friends, once I hear from you. My apologies, Mrs. Luoto, if you are not the Ellen I seek.

Your friend from the past, but not a past friend,
Kermit Bender

"What do you think of that?" she asks the pup, hugging it up into her lap. "Kermit Bender," she laughs. "What do you think of that?" She laughs, kissing the snout and the pup begins great lunging kisses until Ellen slides her to the floor and hands down leftover toast.

All afternoon Ellen hurries through work as she thinks of the letter and the one she will write. When Helmut returns, Ellen, seized with affection for him, takes his jacket from his big scarred hands and pours his coffee.

"How was your trip?"

"The parts for the binder are ordered, but not because that pimply kid wanted my business."

"Why not? They cost enough."

"Not like new machinery. Mine's got to last me out." He looks into his coffee and speaks as though talking to himself. "Sullivan and his son came in, and Pimples was so hot to sell them something he left me with the order book to look up part numbers myself."

She can see the hurt from his slight as he hunches his shoulders. "Kids these days," she says, sipping her coffee.

"Sullivan's son's farming his place now," he says, still looking into the blackness of his coffee.

She doesn't know what to say. What's the sense of comparing things to Sullivan? What son wouldn't stay with those acres of bottom land and that legendary wheat yield? She wants to read the letter to him, but feels cautioned.

It takes three days to compose her letter with all its questions and memories. She puts in some personal information and her snapshot with a grandchild.

"Sadie's knee's busted out again," Helmut says after breakfast.

"I'll poultice it," she tells him. She gathers clean rags and prepares flaxseed, keeping it hot in a double boiler for the trip to the barn. Clamped in her stanchion, Sadie rolls her eyes and shifts her feet, full warning she will not be approached.

"Helmut," Ellen calls.

He enters from the milk house and stands before Sadie, who is calmed, though Helmut offers neither word nor touch.

In five days there is another letter from Gladstone.

"Listen to this, Helmut, a letter from a friend with all kinds of news." She pretends it's her first letter by quoting the coincidental ad about the Holsteins. Helmut stops eating. "Florence Martell's son's a brain surgeon. You remember her? She was still speaking broken English at Cathy's wedding. And Hazel Peterson, my dearest friend in sixth grade. Hazel was widowed last year. She's remarried someone in Florida. Look, here's Kermit's picture with one of his grandchildren. Now that child is the image of Kermit at that age. Amazing." She continues to read the letter, explaining people to Helmut.

"Who is this guy?" Helmut asks.

She's never heard him use the word 'guy.' It annoys her as she explains her childhood friend. Helmut stands before she finishes. "Don't you want to hear the rest of the letter?"

"I don't know the guy," he says, turning away. She hears him stamping on his boots. The pup listens too, leaning against her legs.

Helmut calls the dog, but the animal does not move. She hears him kicking off his boots and he returns to the kitchen with a rope.

"Don't you touch her!" she shouts. "She can't help it if she's not Ginger. You can't choose everything according to how it will work for you."

"What are you talking about?"

"Including me. Uncle Ray saw it. He said you wanted me

because you could see I was strong and healthy, like you pick stock."

He takes a step closer and she wonders if he will hit her, though he's never struck any of them, not even animals. He's looking at the dog pressing against her legs. "She's your dog." He twists the rope in his big hands.

They stand awkwardly. What she's said is between them.

"Did you believe your Uncle Ray?"

Ellen looks up. His eyes, hidden by the depths of brow and cheekbones, are on her. His voice comes rough and low, "Is that what you think?"

"No," she says, touching his arm.

Post-Mortem

LEONARD BEAROR has begun post-mortem preparations when Charlotte Yastremski phones. The instructor requests permission for three students to attend. He can hardly refuse. This is a teaching hospital. Damn her. Damn Yastremski. He wants to finish early and this will add another hour; at least another hour with nursing students, and worse, Yastremski.

He has placed the body on the table when Yastremski enters, and, picking up one of his towels, she asks, "May I cover his face?" She does so without waiting for an answer. This is a hospital procedure, but still, this is his domain, not hers.

The instructor leaves and is back in moments with three young nursing students prepared to watch their first autopsy. Her introduction, as sharp and crisp as her face, is brief. "Dr. Bearor: Miss Lenkner, Miss Sillanpaa, Miss Friday." The three stand together as though some common thread of life connects them. Yastremski assists each into gown and gloves, for they seem incapable of any act, aware of nothing but the naked death on the table before them.

Bearor started this innovation of getting students into gowns and gloves. It happened one day when, on impulse, he invited four medical students to leave the amphitheater to palpate a fibroid tumor. His rather dusty talks became an interaction that excited him and from then on he's involved students, allowing them to weigh organs and record findings. They handle normal lung tissue, feel its sponginess, compare it to the dead-filled spaces of necrotic areas. Apparently Yastremski's heard of these tactile experiences and approves of them for her students.

Bearor checks his Dictaphone, begins his canned speech as he selects instruments from a cabinet. "Before I became a pathologist, I was in private practice," he begins, "but it didn't work out." He barely directs these comments to the students as he positions instruments as orderly as any surgical procedure. "It became my experience that people don't want a doctor to tell them how to lead their lives. As long as death doesn't have them in his teeth, nothing you say motivates them to follow a prescribed regimen."

It irritates Bearor that he feels obliged to justify his switch from private practice. He's good at what he does, but feels a bias, especially from women, that he's down in the bowels of the hospital because he couldn't make it with living, breathing, patients. He comes to work in a loose leather jacket, his sandy hair wet from the shower. Hospital personnel recognize him and smile, though few can place who he is.

"As a pathologist I don't have to listen to patients' idiotic rationalizations," he says. "Here, they don't talk back." There is a ripple of humor on one student's face. The other two stare at him. "I remember one with Buerger's disease. I was an intern at the time, and this fellow had already had one leg amputated. This hospitalization was an attempt to save the other. The guy was a chain smoker and you know how that contributes to the arteriospasm that obstructs circulation. I spent time with him because giving up cigarettes isn't easy. I used to smoke myself."

Bearor picks up the drill, aware of his anger as he presses the extension cord in the outlet. "One day I caught him smoking.

Naturally, he lost the leg." The students remain quiet. Medical students would have barraged him with questions. Bearor checks the drill and savagely jams the bit in the chuck.

In his teaching role Bearor has developed a style, created an atmosphere. By accident he found a few jokes which, when polished and stirred in with some morgue-funnies, became hilarious relief to medical students experiencing their first raw encounter with death. He never fails to use old standbys on a new group.

The students stand in a row, carefully avoiding contact with the autopsy table. Their instructor wearily lowers herself into a seat in the amphitheater. Bearor steps up on the wooden platform, says, "Let me draw your attention to the dark purple on the dorsal aspects of the body. This is a pooling of blood. Gravity's the force now, not the pumping action of a heart." He allows a long pause. "What's wrong with this man?"

They look down at once, then raise puzzled faces to him. He almost laughs. "Whenever you see this," he confides, "you are looking at a bad case of death."

Everything stops. The joke that detonates medical students leaves them frozen. They stand staring as though posing for a time exposure. Yastremski speaks. "Dr. Bearor, these students have been taking care of Martin Yarman," she explains quietly.

Damn women. He's always off on the wrong foot with them. Anger flushes his body. Working rapidly, he slits the skin from the sternum to umbilicus, then across the chest, dissecting through fascia. With rib cutters he cuts through the ribs on both sides and hinges the entire rib cage up over the face. Internal viscera exposed, Martin Yarman becomes a carcass. Bearor glances at his little group and drops a suctioning tube in the body cavity to draw off pooled blood.

It runs dark red in clotted hunks onto the concave, stainless steel table and down the drain. He hears a faint sigh from the group and his anger subsides into hostile satisfaction.

It hadn't been easy moving to the post room. Tools, mostly surgical cast-offs, are impossible. Instead of fighting this economy, he saved his big guns for a bone saw with a vacuum attachment that kept bone dust from clouding the air when he cut off the cap of a skull. His fight for a hoist to convey a body from the refrigerator to the post-mortem table seemed futile. His department head stubbornly refused to recognize the need, actually prided himself on his ability to lift bodies directly from the refrigerator tray to the table. Murphy always did it himself, those occasional times when he gave one of his forensic lectures to a full house.

Then a wonderful thing happened. Two elderly orderlies, lifting a woman to the top of the tray, accidentally dropped her, cracking the head like a coconut. That very day, Murphy lifted an obese woman from the tray and slipped on the wet floor. Still in his arms, she lay on him, a naked dead weight, as he struggled to get up. The attending interns and medical students, struck dumb, watched his helpless flailing until he roared, "Get her off, you goddamned bastards!" The hoist was ordered and in place within the week.

"This man could be alive today," Bearor says. "Mr. Yarman ignored diet, doubled his insulin when he drank, and reaped all the consequences of atherosclerosis." He's aware of the rasp in his voice, the sound of anger. The students move closer together. Bearor gave up private practice because of anger, because of patients who would not follow the rules. As an intern he had slapped a patient. The man had already lost a leg and Bearor went out of his way to make sure he understood about cigarettes. He caught him smoking. It happened so quickly, the slap coming hard and swift, the hand of his mother.

He feels the group solidify against him. One lifts her head a moment, seemingly physically supported on two sides by her friends. She's upset and her voice shakes. "He didn't reject. His doctor didn't teach him. He –"

"So it's his doctor's fault?" Bearor cuts in. "Let me tell you one on the nurses. Yesterday I posted a little old lady (actually she'd been a great hulk of a woman) and do you know what she died of? Grapefruit juice!" He gives a short laugh. "I found grapefruit juice in her lungs. She drowned. How do you suppose that happened?"

They look up, stricken.

"The nurses were feeding her fluids with a syringe and she wasn't swallowing. She was aspirating it! The chart stated she had moist rales for a week before she finally died. Really, before the nurses killed her." Bearor glances at Yastremski. "I'm sure you teach students to withhold fluids when the patient can't swallow."

He can't see Yastremski's response. She may have shrugged, but he feels her watching and he sees the students pressed together. "Here's the prize. This old guy comes in for elective surgery for tic doulourex, which incidentally, he's lived with for eleven years. He dies four weeks later with tetanus. The only mark on him was an inflamed injection site on his butt."

"The nurses gave him tetanus?"

"Sure. Figure it out. About a fourth of the population have tetanus spores in their feces. Harmless enough in the gastrointestinal tract. This poor devil couldn't get himself clean lying in bed and some nurse comes along and doesn't clean his buttocks good enough before giving the shot. The needle introduces the spore nice and deep. Incubation period's about four weeks. He didn't get tetanus outside the hospital."

Yastremski laughs, but her voice is hard. "Come now, doctor, the incubation period has been known to be longer. Besides, you've left out all of what might have gone on in surgery. You're giving some valuable information, but I wish you would quit thumping these students."

The same student raises her head. "Dr. Bearor, Mr. Yarman didn't understand about his diet and insulin. He couldn't speak English."

It's time to systematically excise each organ. He puts the students to work with weighing and recording their findings. He takes samplings of tissue from each organ for the specimen bottles. For twenty minutes they work, and his anger gradually drains.

He had slapped the man, knocking the cigarette from his mouth, never considering consequences. There could have been a law suit. He could have lost his internship. The patient sobbed. He didn't care if they took the other leg. Life was over. Relieved, Bearor had not really listened. Nothing came of it.

The students, happy with their grams and kilograms, record in the Dictaphone. When they finish, one asks, "Could you get gas gangrene from human feces, too?"

"Certainly. You're thinking about that patient who died here a couple of weeks ago?"

The tall girl nods.

"After he died they put him in the refrigerator and when I came to do the post he was so blown up I couldn't get him out." Bearor can see that picture going around in their heads. Medical students, too cool to register horror, would have laughed.

"You couldn't get him out?" It was the middle one again. "Didn't you have someone to help you?"

"No, it was around ten-thirty at night."

"Oh, I don't think you should work alone down here." The

same student glances anxiously around the room.

"No, you shouldn't," another says and they all look at him with concern. Speechless, Bearor pauses, and pulls himself away.

It's time to do the skull, and for the first time Martin Yarman's face is exposed. The students seem startled. They've forgotten, never really realized, he supposes. "Perhaps you've had enough for one day," he suggests, thinking one of them will certainly faint and delay him for hours.

They interpret this as a kindness; he can see that. Their faces reflect appreciation and a determination to see it through. He carefully covers the face as best he can.

Bearor explains that, legally, there must not only be a permit for autopsy, but a special one for the head. It will be their responsibility as nurses to assure the family that the head will show no evidence of the procedure. He will cut behind the hair line. The marks will not be visable.

The sound of sawing through bone, not unlike that of any Skil saw, always evokes the memory of his tree being killed. His tree house, his retreat. He asks one of the students to hold some of the hair aside. He had imagined the tree loved him, wanted him in its arms. At night, after his sister's death, he often ran to the tree because of fear or loneliness. There was always a soft stirring of leaves, even when the air was still. Up in its branches, he felt the flow of its love for him.

He begins to cut behind Martin Yarman's left ear and has to shift his position. The saw shrieks.

He had to run from the savage sound. That relentless force killing his tree. The sound's still unbearable, the ripping, the voice of his mother because he had broken the rules.

Bearor completes the cut and lays the skull cap aside. Yastremski has left her seat and is standing at the side, watching.

The middle student is ashen. "Tell me the names of the suture lines I've cut through," Bearor demands.

She looks blank.

"Come, come, think! You certainly must know them."

She floods scarlet.

Yastremski's rippling laugh tumbles over them. "I don't think Dr. Bearor really expected you to remember the suture lines, Miss Sillanpaa. He's just done a very clever thing. You were becoming pale, so he purposely embarrassed you with a tough question." She laughs again. "It got blood to your brain."

The students look at him with appreciation. The middle one, Miss Sillanpaa, resembles his sister. Annie, who believed everything he said, forgave his tricks, trusted, even as the pail spilled water over her.

Robert, the orderly, opens the door shouting, "Dr. Bearor, look what's coming!" He holds back the heavy door and they see a green pick-up easing back to the loading dock. Though a poorly secured tarpaulin conceals some of it, the unmistakable end of a rusting casket sticks up over the end of the tailgate.

There's a general gasp from the group. Yastremski's the first to collect herself. "Why are they bringing an old casket here? Patients' windows look down on that dock!"

Bearor can't run out with his blood stained gown and gloves. "My God, Robert. Get out there and ask what the hell they think they're doing."

Robert leaves. The door whumps behind him, shutting off their view.

"Someone get the door."

Yastremski jerks it open and they see Robert talking to two men in the cab. He jogs back to their room, paper in hand. "They're from up north. From Amity."

"Hold the paper, Robert. Over here so I can read it." Bearor holds his gloved hands to the side, crooks his neck and brings his face close to the document. "It's from the sheriff, says the lady was exhumed because there's evidence her husband might have poisoned her. They want tissue studies. The idiots!" Bearor rushes past them and kicks open the glass door at the dock. His gown whips in the wind, his hair straightens. He leans to the cab window, yelling above the wind.

"You can't bring that here. Get it out! What? Well, call Dr. Murphy from a phone booth. He'll tell you what to do, but you can't bring it here!"

It's not possible to hear the men in the pick-up, but apparently they intend to stay.

Bearor grasps the side-view mirror as though to fling them away. "This is a hospital, you idiots. Get out of here!" He kicks savagely at the side of the cab.

The motor starts. It dies. Bearor raises his arms, an enraged prophet as the wind tears at his gown and hair. The pick-up starts up the steep grade, bumping its cargo from side to side.

Bearor returns. The ponderous door swings shut. "From Amity. That's all the way from Aroostook County." They look at each other. Where it starts he'll never know, but they explode with laughter. It lasts until they are weak, and erupts again. It includes them all, even Yastremski. In the warmth of laughter, they all but hug.

Bearor returns to the final finish-up tasks of putting the organ remains and tissues in the body cavity. These are pocketed loosely before he sews the skin surfaces together. When he spills in brain fragments, there is a small wail from Sillanpaa. "Not his brains."

Bearor looks at her.

"Not his brains. Not in with the intestines." She's shored up by her classmates, her trembling mouth still softly forming the protest.

In all his memory he can not remember anyone crying at a post. Everything stops. They all look at him, even Yastremski. For a moment he doesn't know what to do. He looks at Sillanpaa, so like Annie. "It doesn't matter now," he says gently. She accepts this, nodding her head as though giving him permission to proceed. He looks at their faces. "After we finish, let's go for coffee. I want you to tell me about Martin Yarman."

Shard

LIKE ALL her father's buildings, the empty cottage was built of stone. Set apart on the mountain overlooking the valley, one could see a blue ribbon of loch at the bottom. The cottage was for a hired person and had not been lived in since Sandy MacKinnan left for America. There were but two rooms and the windows small because of continuous southwest winds that blew across the North Atlantic and the rocky barren land. Her father's croft was poor. Only the land at the head of a glen had scant rich soil deposited from the mountains. Heavy rain restricted the crop to oats, potatoes, and barley, but the loch supplied trout and there were salmon in the sea. As a girl, she remembered deer and grouse, but it had been a long time.

Mary sat on a stone and looked at the cottage. In the old days there had been two shaggy-horned cattle in the glen. In late summer they roamed the lower slopes where purple heather bloomed. There had been sheep. As a child she sat on this outcropping of rock with her brother, who told stories of the people who had lived in the carse beyond the rise of MacKenzie's croft, and of the Ice Age glaciers that chiseled the Highlands.

"I'll say goodbye," she said. "I'll not be coming back." It surprised her that she had spoken, that she felt a loss. Her family was gone. She had sold the croft, locked the main house for the last time. In a few months she would start her education to become a doctor at the University of Edinburgh.

Mary fingered the ring of keys, recalling the many times she'd watched her father putting them away in the locked drawer of his desk. Today she had gone through that desk, and every locked compartment of the house, and found nothing, nothing worthy of lock and key. It was strange how voices of those gone had come to her as she parted from the house. Touching the carved back of her grandmother's rocker, the old woman's ancient Gaelic came to her as crisp and clear as in Mary's childhood. Her brother's voice had always been with her. She was eleven when Adam was lost at sea. She would not let his spirit rest but conjured him up, talked to him until he answered. Her father had said, "I'll have ye locked up at Aberdeen if I hear another word."

When she emptied the great desk, she could hear her father. It made her turn, half expecting to see his thin frame in the doorway, his accusing eyes watching. He would suspect she sought something of her mother's, a ring, a picture. Since she was eight, nothing remained that spoke of a mother who deserted them. Sometimes, in those first days, Mary thought she saw her mother and would run from room to room catching an aroma, a whisper of movement, a filmy glimpse. "It is yourself you deceive," her father said. She tried to weep secretly, but once when he came upon her his savage voice hurled, "She had no love for either of you. Has there ever been a word from her? Put her from your mind."

"Why did she leave us?" she asked Adam. They had been sitting here, and Adam could only shake his head.

Mary looked down at the ring of keys she would soon leave at the land office in the village. She had labeled them carefully, all but the cottage key. The cottage lay some distance away, but she decided to check and label the last key. It was a pleasant walk. June in the Highlands was the best of months. She might have stayed until her school term began, but the agent had been anxious to accommodate some English tourists. As she drew near the cottage, she felt a great sadness. She and Adam had played here as children. At sixteen, he could no longer bear the harshness of their father. Often at night she'd heard the whip on Adam's back. From the time their mother left, he'd done the work of a hired person and many mornings she found him asleep over his books. At eleven he failed the exam for senior school, the only path to the universities.

The sun was well over the castle by the time she reached the cottage. One of the windows was shattered, as though some giant had heaved a great field stone. No one had gained entry, for the jagged shards at the base of the window had not been disturbed. She unlocked the door without hesitation. The mice had chewed the soap and candle, but nothing seemed out of place. The tins for biscuits, sugar, and flour were neatly lined on a shelf. The bare cot held the folded blankets last used by Sandy MacKinnan.

Mary walked to the window, curious to find what object had been hurled, but could find nothing. The force had come from outside, for the glass lay everywhere. Perhaps it had been Friday's strong wind, carrying the deluge of rain, but the dark drapes were dry and there was no trace of water stains on the wall beneath the window or on the floor. It had happened last night or today, when no wind blew.

The largest shard of glass leaned against the wall, carrying a blinding reflection of the sun. 'This is not possible,' Mary thought. 'The sun can not shine through a building. It's reflected from something in this room.' Behind her the cellar door's brass knob reflected the blood-red of the sun. It was not the dull brass of disuse, but shiny from years of a hand's polishing. She grasped the knob and felt a great shudder go through the cottage.

Inspector Brant watched his friend laboring up the hill to the cottage. "Where's Mary now?"

"Staying at the Inn. My Janice is with her."

"She doesn't know yet what was found?"

"Nay, but she was certain her mother was down in that cellar. That's why she came runnin' to us. She didn't go down."

"Now, how would she know?"

"She said it was a feeling from the cottage."

"Is she in bad shape?"

"I don't think so. She said, 'I knew Mother would not leave us.'"

"Are you going to tell her what else was found?"

"It'll have to come out. She'll have to be told Sandy MacKinnan was there too, shot dead."

"And her mother?"

"I don't think she need know the details of the murder. It's clear her father did it. Odd this happened now, with him just put to rest."

"How did he kill her?"

"I'll let you guess. You knew the man. Church Elder twenty years, strapped his boy regular, saying we are sinners in the hands of an angry God, knew his Bible. Think, man. It took all his poor wife's strength to protect her kids, but a life like that finally wore her down. I don't wonder that she found comfort with Sandy MacKinnan. How do you think he would do it?"

Inspector Brant winced. "He didn't stone her."

"Aye, Inspector, that he did."

A Question of Performance

IT WAS in morning report when this started. Our director of Nursing Service was saying, "I can easily respond to the problems that have eventuated because of the timing. We can now regard the totality of the activity." She always speaks this way. The rest of Nursing Service are almost as bad, and that includes me, because I've given up and play the game.

Quimby, supervisor of 5 North and South, sat fingering her unlighted cigarette. We'd been in report almost an hour before her intensity became anticipatory fondling. Quimby's crazy. I consider this factual because it comes directly from students who, on a sliding scale, are the most sane of hospital personnel, unless you want to include housekeeping.

Quimby's harmless enough. She has a psychiatric background, but patients on the neurology unit are too sick to pay much attention. She is a shock to students. One day last month she invited four affiliating students to her apartment for pie and coffee. The moment they walked in she asked if they wanted pie, and because they weren't decisive she withdrew the offer. She ate hers and though the evening dragged on for three more hours, she didn't offer pie again. Whenever a student shifted her position, Quimby stopped all conversation to ask, "Why did you move? Let's examine what you are feeling at this moment." The first student was Crystal, who flushed scarlet and shifted again. "There you go!" Quimby cried out. Crystal rigidified so solidly she had leg cramps in the night.

I glanced around at the others who, like myself, were drifting. Two of the younger supervisors struggled to focus, but most had switched to automatic pilot.

We're all supervisors of special units, but rotate to get a different perspective on how a unit is functioning. When there's trouble, one of us will show up with a notebook and pencil and stalk about the unit with a perpetual look of concern. It generally adds to the insecurity of the staff. Of course, we achieve nothing.

As I said, the director had just stated, "We can now regard the totality of the activity." I was nodding agreeably when she asked, "Do you think a week will suffice?"

I considered, sucking in my cheeks as I do to convey deep thought. I glanced at the others who gave no clue concerning subject matter. It was obvious I had an assignment, so, hazarding a guess that a week might mean rushing me, I said, "At least a week."

The director smiled approvingly.

I smiled as we adjourned, knowing it would all be clarified when I could get hold of Rainbow's minutes.

Our secretary, Rainbow, is a genius. On the edge of her chair, she glides her great dark eyes from speaker to speaker as she re-defines our meeting. Though English is her second language, the minutes come pithy from her pen. They look good for state accreditation, amazing us with our accomplishments.

I found I was to spend a week of nights on 5 North to gather evidence of the suitability of a Miss Ellie Milanski's performance, especially the appropriateness of her language.

Miss Milanski is charge night nurse on 5 North. She can't be over five feet two, with the complexion and delicacy of a Dresden doll. Her hair's in a thick blond braid bouncing down her back.

Monday night I showed up on 5 North, before report, and found Milanski doing rounds with a team leader from the evening shift. I watched them progressing down the darkened hall, saw Milanski bend to scratch notes on her clip board, her face illuminated by floor night lights.

I introduced myself, saying I was on a routine unit evaluation and would probably be there no longer than a week.

"Does that mean you'll work in a pinch?"

"I might," I said.

She squinted up at me and I felt the quick scanning judgment one sees in children.

I found nothing to report that first night. She did receive one personal call, but it was from her father who has a janitorial position at *The Onward* magazine building. Milanski handled her staff efficiently; her procedures were above reproach. I wondered what had precipitated this surveillance. It was her morning report that made me prick up my ears.

"He sleeps *au naturale*, so watch out. He flings off his covers for hypos," she said, speaking of a new admission.

"That should be exciting," the head nurse said flatly, flicking to the next page of her notes.

"He's strictly gag material," Milanski said, "make sure your breakfast's settled."

I could tell the head nurse had swung her head to see my reaction. I doodled on my note pad, keeping my face blank. Had the head nurse put Milanski on report?

The next five patients were reported in professional detail. Then she reached Mrs. Row.

"Don't let that snotty Quimby assign students to Mrs. Row today. She's dying and knows it."

"What do you mean?" the head nurse asked.

"Death's big in the curriculum these days," Milanski said, "everyone elbowing to share the experience, crowding the patient to spill his guts. It's the new thrill, like sex ten years ago. 'How do you feel about dying, Mrs. Jones? Hand me a tissue, I'm here to cry with you, but I can't stay long, I have a one-thirty class.'"

The head nurse put down her pencil. "You haven't heard anything like that, have you?"

"No, but a student did work on a patient, did get him talking about his death, and did leave him to go to class. That was last week. Remember Mr. Anders?"

The head nurse nodded and picked up her pencil. "I'll keep Mrs. Row out of student hands," she promised.

I watched Milanski leave the hospital. She had pulled on a leather jacket over her braid which hung down below like a tail swishing across her rump.

The second night went as before. I was impressed with Milanski, but again she surprised me in morning report.

"Mrs. Bond has all this green garbage, this crap, coming out of that wound. What a stink."

"Can't you be a little more explicit?" the head nurse asked.

"She should be in isolation," Milanski continued. "Get Dr. Maylee to get it cultured. I put some in a culture tube. All we need is his order."

The head nurse laid down her pencil. "I'll ask, but Doctor Maylee is reluctant about suggestions from nurses."

"Unbutton your uniform three notches," Milanski advised.

When report was over, the head nurse said, "Miss Milanski, I need to ask you about an incident reported to me by Miss Quimby."

I stood up to leave.

Milanski reached up and tugged my skirt. "Stay, Ma, you're going to know about it anyways. You should hear my side."

I sat. So that was what she called me? Why Ma? My age, I supposed.

"Did you call Miss Quimby 'stupid?'" the head nurse asked.

Milanski laughed. "No, but you're close."

We waited.

Milanski sighed. "I was just going off duty and stopped in Shirley Bell's room to give her the new ointment for her pressure sore. There was Quimby, hot on one of her psychological digs. Quimby was saying, 'I wish you would be honest with yourself, Shirley. I think you have a void in your life.' I pushed Quimby into the hall and said, 'Certainly Shirley has a void. She's paraplegic, divorced, and now she has this bedsore. I think you must have a void in your head.'"

We three sat in silence. They were waiting for me. I looked up. "Even if it's a reasonable deduction," I said, "that's no way to speak to Miss Quimby."

I found Quimby in our office stuggling to finish her cigarettes before the supervisor's meeting. "Have you got enough to nail her to the floor?" she asked. For a moment I could visualize Quimby doing just that.

"I'm giving it one more night," I said watching the jerk of her eyes. "Sometimes you give me the shivers, Quimby," This seemed to please her.

On the fifth night I concluded my assignment. Everything broke loose around two in the morning and was compounded by three admissions. We had interns everywhere and Milanski orchestrated. One patient was admitted for "fainting spells" and when she fainted again, Milanski tried to check her pupils. The patient resisted and screwed her eyes shut. "So much for fainting," Milanski whispered, moving on to the next admission, who hadn't been able to sleep. Since she was to be admitted the following day, she thought she might as well come on in. She howled for a sleeping pill and the intern ordered seconal. Milanski looked at her chart. "This woman's been on thirty mg. of Dalmane for twelve years!" she told the intern. "The seconal isn't going to touch her. Better leave another order if you expect any sleep tonight."

The third patient had come in for status epilepticus and had been treated in the emergency room. Suddenly his seizures began again. "My God, what do we do now?" one intern asked the other. They both looked at Milanski. "What do you do when someone's already on Dilantin and still's convulsing?" one cried. Milanski picked up the phone. "I don't know. I'll ask my mom." She took a deep breath and got the resident out of bed. There was no let up, but Milanski stayed on top of things. She even put me to work. I changed I.V. bags, started an I.V. on one of the admissions, and sat with Elizabeth Ann who was being visited by space men in football suits.

During morning report, Milanski said, "That must have been one hell of an I.V. Ma put in because Mr. Crisp got out of bed, walked into the wall, fell flat, fought like a bull while we were getting him back to bed, but the I.V.'s still running."

I tried to look modest and doodled on my pad, but the 5 North staff turned to me with a different look and my heart pounded. After report I told Milanski I wouldn't be coming back on nights.

She smiled. "Heck, you were just beginning to have a good time."

I found Quimby at her desk waiting to go into report. Her head was down.

"What's the matter?" I asked.

"I find that looking at people saps my energy," she said, "so, I must just not look at them."

I read my lengthy report on Miss Milanski. Everyone was impressed as I concluded: "She established protocols to assure an environment conducive to optimum restoration and maintenance of client's normal abilities to meet basic needs, and implemented care according to appropriate priorities of needs."

"What about her language?" the director asked.

I was ready for that. "Tersely cogent," I said. "I suppose she gets it from her father. You do realize he's with *The Onward*?"

Our director would never part the pages of a progressive liberal publication, even to explore its masthead, but I saw her brain click warning. She wasn't about to step into a mess. I glanced at Rainbow. A little smile jerked at her upper lip and her eyes, moist with approval, slipped over her notes. I felt the night's fatigue slip away.

The Other Side

HOWARD WAS amazed at the number of times his name came up. Certainly one might expect it right after death, but now, ten years later, he was still zeroing in on what people were saying, what they remembered about him. He found it a nuisance. He'd gotten into his restructuring, or so he thought, was redefining his past life and suddenly, wham, he had to be present for those words. The technology astounded him. He was there, visualizing living people at the beginning of any spoken word that referred directly to him.

At first it dizzied him. Bodyless souls were not subject to vertigo, but new as he was to this existence, he could think of no closer description. Howard could remember every visit. That was another remarkable thing, every visit including his reaction. With no effort he could run the experience through his mind, like a tape, even the first time with Margo dancing alone in their living room. Eyes closed, arms raised in ballroom position, she moved sensuously to Nat King Cole's Lost April. He'd watched, enthralled, though it was a bit embarrassing, for obviously she fantasized the dance with him. It was their song. Moving closer, he'd considered trying to make some contact, but when he saw the tears he'd fled. It was easy to do. He didn't have to stick around if he didn't want to, that much he'd learned. A kind of turning away and he was back in the comfort of his void.

Now, here he was back with Margo and two people he didn't know.

"That movie was in sixty-six," the man says. "I remember Howard wanted to see it because the lead guy looked so much like him, every one thought so. Naturally, Howard didn't say that, just said it was a film we shouldn't miss."

"Who is this man? He seems to know me," Howard mutters.

"How can you remember it was in sixty-six?" Margo says.

"Easy," the man replies. "That was the year Jessica and I divorced."

"Jessica?" Howard muses. "Then he has to be Ronald Nolton, Jessica Nolton's husband. I wouldn't know him. He's aged."

"No more than Margo."

"Jessica, where did you come from?"

"Hush. I want to hear this."

"Can they hear us?"

"No, but I can't hear if you keep on jabbering."

They watch Margo walk the length of her living room. "It seems so long ago," Margo says. "I remember the actor was Sterling Ford. He and Howard could have been brothers."

"Maybe we were," a voice says. "I was adopted."

"Who's speaking?" Howard says.

"Sterling Ford, naturally," Jessica says. "Honestly, Howard, it's been ten years. Haven't you learned anything?"

"I never stick around," Howard says. "No one told me."

"Aren't you curious? Heavens, I knew the limitations of this existence the first week."

"It didn't interest me," Howard says.

"You mean you just float around here? It figures, Howard.

You were always so self-absorbed."

"Hearing people talk about you is a bother," Howard says.

"If you'd been a movie star, you'd know what bother really is," Sterling Ford says. "I have to be present every time my name comes up. It doesn't matter that they never knew me, and now with all those reruns. Fame exacts a terrible price."

"What's the point?" Howard says. "I can't see any point."

"Typical Howard. You never got the point of living either and now you're one hopeless soul. You'll pay for it. The next time around, you'll pay."

"Wait a minute," Sterling Ford says. "You two can chat anytime, but I may have to leave. I've got questions. You say you looked like me?"

"Spitting image," Jessica says.

"What about your parents?"

"Never knew my real ones," Howard says.

"Now that's interesting," Sterling Ford says, "because my real name was Harold; and Howard, get it? Sounds like brothers."

"My real mother was a dancer," Howard says.

"Not quite accurate," says a voice.

"Who are you?" Howard says.

"Howard, give an educated guess," Jessica says. "You just said 'mother,' you said, 'my real mother.'"

"Mother, is that you?" Howard says.

"Of course," his mother says. "I wondered when one of you would call me up, but you were both dull children."

"Well, I'll be," says Sterling Ford.

"As I was saying," the mother says, "It's not quite accurate that I was a dancer. I served drinks in this fancy nightclub and my costume was a dazzler. Every hour the girls on drinks formed a chorus line on stage with high kicks and bounces while the band played Gait Parisian. It was a lot of laughs because most of us couldn't kick two feet off the ground."

"Why are you telling us this?" Sterling Ford asks.

"How long have you been here?" his mother asks.

"Eight years."

"You see what I mean about being dull, Jessica? Eight years and he still doesn't know you have to tell the truth and even correct another soul's misconception about you."

"He's Einstein compared to Howard," Jessica says.

"Was that a chance reference to me?"

"I'm so sorry, Professor Einstein. I know better, I was just carried away."

"I'll leave, then. Sounds crowded." They hear a whoosh.

"What was that?" Howard says.

"That was you-know-who, taking his leave," Jessica says.

"I still don't get the point," Howard says.

Jessica sighs. "My perception is that we're supposed to be getting ready to live."

"That's the way I figure it," the mother says. "And if you two boys are going to diddle your time away, you won't be prepared at all."

"Prepared?" Howard cries, "I don't want to live. I like it here. I'm perfectly content."

"We all are," Jessica says. "It's not that easy. We have to know ourselves when we go back, or we won't improve in the least when we get there. It takes work, I'll tell you. Dedication, and we never know when our time will come."

"What good does it do to know ourselves?" Sterling Ford asks. "I didn't know anything about my previous existence before my last earth life."

"Oh yes, you did," Jessica says. "Wordsworth was pretty much on track when he said, 'The soul that rises with us, our life song hath had elsewhere its setting…'"

"Mind if I correct that quotation?" Wordsworth says, "it's our life's star.'"

"Oh, I'm sorry," Jessica cries. "That's the second time I've pulled a soul in."

"I don't mind," Wordsworth says. "I'm not called up much these days. Really, it's my pleasure."

"What amazes me is that your soul hasn't been replanted," Jessica says. "You must have been here over a hundred years."

"A hundred and forty, to be exact," Wordsworth says. "I'm negotiating, attempting to compile evidence that I'm worthy of slipping off the wheel of life, so to speak. These things take time. The poem you attempted to quote is just one point in what I hope is substantial evidence…"

"I would think so," Jessica says. "I'm a great fan of yours and I would think that from 'Intimations of Immortality' alone there would be no question."

"You're very kind."

"Can I get hold of a copy?" Howard asks.

"Forget it, Howard, you wouldn't understand a word of it," Jessica says.

"Perhaps she means you're not ready," Wordsworth soothes.

"Maybe some of your other stuff?" Howard asks.

"Much of it is very dull," Wordsworth says. "I think you might enjoy Sam Coleridge more."

"You said his name. Does that mean he's here?"

"No, we lost him twenty-seven years ago."

"I hate to butt in," Sterling Ford says, "but I want to ask Mother if she has any advice before I get pulled away."

"Well, son, you and Howard should know that if you don't do well now, it will make your life that much more difficult. So, don't waste time. We never know when we'll be called. And Harold, put in a complaint. Sterling Ford's not your real name, so get that fixed. You're Harold Pappajohn. With that name, you shouldn't be bothered."

"Gee, thanks, Mom," Harold Pappajohn says.

"Yeah, thanks," echoes his brother.

Visiting Mother This Summer

SO MUCH unchanged. I lie awake listening for voices, long gone. The breakers, the owls, the ceaseless melancholy whistle of pines, pull me back. I suppose it's the same with everyone. I feel small, tucked-in, with a sharp anticipation of morning. Near dawn I wake to the ghost-back of Caesar and lie still, hoping to hear him again.

As we sit at breakfast, it seems we should be waiting for Mr. Orloff and Igor. Mother moves painfully to the piano and begins to play. It's badly out of tune. She winces and folds her hands in her lap. "The spring fogs ruin the piano's tune."

I laugh. "I'll bet you haven't had it tuned since Mr. Orloff."

"You remember him?"

"Why wouldn't I? He came every summer."

"What do you remember?" She looks almost young as she sits straight-backed, hands still folded in her lap.

"I remember you said winter-dry and spring fogs ruined your piano. You told Father Mr. Orloff had to come." Mother continues to look, waiting for me to go on.

"The years I remember most must have been when he brought along his little dog. Remember Igor? He stayed under the piano. I can see him now. Not a hair, not a movement suggested he was in any way approachable." I watched mother's slow, inward smile. "Didn't Mr. Orloff always ride out in Matt Peterson's truck?"

"Yes, he did and just at this time of year. I usually had you pick violets for the table." She rises stiffly and stands at the window near the drive, just as I remember her. Caesar would bellow hysterically when he heard Matt's truck and in a few moments we would see Mr. Orloff coming up the trail with Igor stepping daintily behind.

"It was really Igor I noticed," I say. "Mr. Orloff always seemed so ancient. Father laughed at his old European way of dressing. That black suit and dark tie gave him such a formal look, and his hair, I remember it was just long enough to cover the tips of his ears and Father claimed he cut it himself."

"I'm surprised you remember so much," Mother says, turning from the window and moving to the kitchen. "Why don't we have coffee in here, in the sun?"

I hesitate, not wanting to lose the unexpected flood of memory. I think of Mr. Orloff turning to me with his dark look. "Igor has come to play with you," he said, his voice deeply accented in unfamiliar cadence. "He's been looking forward to this visit."

Under the piano, Igor and I eyed each other. Ears flat-back, eyes enormous, he kept one front paw curved close to his chest as though ready to thrust, in a spin, away from me. When I lay down he watched me as he might a dangerous snake.

"Aren't you coming?" Mother calls.

I move to the door. "Isn't it strange I should remember so many details of that dog?"

"Not so strange," Mother says. "If you try, you might remember more."

"Weren't Mr. Orloff's tools laid out on a blue cloth on the piano bench, and didn't he always take off his coat and turn up the cuffs of his white shirt?"

Mother smiles.

"I longed to touch that little dog. I would inch my body closer and closer. I can almost feel how the rug scratched my arms and legs."

Mother laughs and begins pouring coffee.

Mr. Orloff had been checking pitch and chords with his tuning forks when I became aware of him. Without lifting my head from the rug I turned to look up. I cannot say his expression was different, but we exchanged a long moment, an intimacy I didn't understand. "Igor, you must learn to risk if you are to find love," he said gently before returning to his work.

Apparently I became bored and went off to play, for when I returned they were at lunch, discussing music. There seemed a harmony, a flow of words between them without dominance or demand. One spoke and the other's body inclined forward as gently as marsh grass. I watched the delicate weaving flow of their movements, so unlike my father's and brother's bursts for supremacy.

"Your lunch is in the oven," Mother murmured.

I took my place, but their attention did not include me. Secretly, I looked at Mr. Orloff's damaged hand. The thumb and index fingers were gone, the three remaining fingers brutally shortened. He'd been a pianist before the accident. They rose and moved to the piano where Mother started a German Lieder, simple and sad. I wished she would show off one of her hard pieces.

Mr. Orloff began to sing, his voice quavering, thin. "Aus meinen grossen Schmerzen," and Mother joined, "mach ich die kleinen Lieder." I started to leave. "Don't go," Mother called. "It's time to take Mr. Orloff back to town."

I walked ahead to the car and cooped Igor up before getting

in. All the way to town I held him tightly, singing to him, in the back seat. When I lowered my face to his muzzle he turned his head away, but we remained cheek to jaw.

When I was old enough to know about Mr. Orloff's accident, he had already died. Illya Orloff had been the pianist in Chicago's Blackstone Theater. One night, in 1917, he was beaten in his apartment by three unknown men who chopped off his fingers. Though he was Russian, they had mistaken him for a German.

Mother and I sip coffee. Suddenly she puts down her cup and goes to her desk. I see her holding a photograph which she passes to me. "Do you recognize anyone?"

It's an enlargement of a group at a picnic. Mother, no more than eighteen, is in a white dress. I see the ends of a large bow holding back her hair. "I've never seen this picture of you, Mother. How beautiful."

"No, no. I wanted you to see someone else."

I study the unknown men and women, and suddenly I'm drawn to a man I've seen before. Unmindful of the camera's eye, he is looking at my mother. Startled, I remember something of the depth of darkness she must see as she smiles into his eyes.

Plastics

DR. MASON hustles to the lounge, his two associates at heel. These three, always duking it out publicly, make it unnecessary for Carol, who's just finished scrubbing on a five hour by-pass, to make a pretense of sleeping.

"You can't have huge silicone boob transplants on a woman with narrow shoulders," Dr. Durkin huffs.

Mason stops. He's a solid man, not quite short, and in his scrubs his build suggests a cylinder from shoulder to knee. Stiff black hair sprouts from his shirt. The pants he wears, like the ones he'd worn all through his residency, have a crotch that's well below his knees. In defense he lifts a brow, saying, "This lady's a minister's wife and none of the boys uptown would do anything for her."

"She'd be better off," Durkin snorts. "My God, Mason, don't you know anything about aesthetics?" and Barker, with rarely a thought of his own but who speaks as though Durkin's utterance has just occurred to him, says, "Never put big boobs on a woman with narrow shoulders."

Mason rubs his eyes, his ploy for time, and looks over at Carol. "None of the boys uptown would touch her. I thought she deserved better," he says, as though appealing to a judge. Carol, who hasn't the faintest notion what the woman looks like, responds with a sympathetic nod.

Carol's been a first scrub for ten years. All the big-time surgeons ask for her, but she's rarely with the plastics team unless it's something serious like a bad accident. Mason learned she liked ballet, and several years ago he asked her out. She refused. Three months later he tried again with tickets for a New York production. She turned him down again. In both cases, she simply thanked him and refused. No smacking her forehead or moan of regret that she had a conflict. Though she's always happy to talk to him in the lounge, he's never tried again.

Mason's two associates burst away to the locker room and, wanting no more criticism, Mason slumps in a lounger across from Carol. "Elective surgery's expensive," he says, "but it's what she's always wanted. I pointed out that everyone would notice, but she's been wearing large padded bras for years."

Carol nods and smiles, "I'm sure she'll be very pleased."

Mason is happy. Alone with Carol, he eases back in the lounger that elevates his feet. "Suppose you were on that five hour by-pass this morning?"

Carol moans, "I was. My legs are killing me."

"Varicosities?"

"Oh, sure. Ten years of this. What can you expect? Have to face it and get out of surgery."

His heart skips. He could use an office nurse for patient teaching. One he can train to scrub on delicate plastics. Cautiously, he ventures, "You could scrub on minor cases. More change of pace."

"Appys? Hernias? Circumcisions?" she says, her mouth twisting in distaste. "I'd be bored out of my skull."

Mason rubs his eyes. There goes his little bid to have her work for him. He wonders again why she turned him down.

He knows he's no Don Juan, but there are women who've made overtures. Janet on CB4 has suggested, in fact rather pointedly, that they have things in common and the head nurse on 3 North never gets a team leader to assist him, but drops everything to accompany him on rounds.

"I guess I'm lucky," he says. My legs have the circulatory competency of an elephant."

She laughs and he loves the way she closes her eyes as though there's not room for mouth and eyes to be open at the same time. "What kind of options have you been thinking of?" he asks.

"Yesterday, I'm over on 3 West looking the place over because I know they're crying for staff. Eisley, down in personnel, said the assistant head nurse opening is mine if I want it. I know staffing problems stem from the head nurse because Arquet was a class mate of mine and the moment she became a senior she started in on underclassmen. Never changed. She sees me on the floor, guesses why I'm there. 'Something happen in surgery?' she says. 'Varicosities,' I say and she pinches her face up like she's thinking, 'I'll bet.'"

"You don't want to work with a person like that," Mason says, thrilled with this confidence.

She closes her eyes. "I know 3 West isn't a healthy place, but worse, I hate leaving the O.R." He can see she's holding back tears and he wants to take her hand and tell her he'll take care of everything.

Durkin and Barker, natty in street clothes, come out of the locker room. Three years ago they were subjected to the details of Mason's frustrated infatuation with Carol. Supportive at first, they changed tactics after Carol's second rejection. "Drop her," Durkin said. "Plenty more where she came from."

Durkin's married to a woman from Larchmont, a graduate of

Oberlin who'd been a child viola prodigy. Barker's single, doesn't have a steady girl, but rubber stamps Durkin's pronouncement with, "Plenty of fish in the sea." Mason has stopped obsessing about Carol, but now he sees the look in his associates' eyes; Durkin sighting down his long aristocratic nose, while Barker struggles to convey a similar message. Mason squirms. Being the most recognized of all the area's plastic surgeons is not enough. He needs their approval. With a whump he collapses the leg elevation of his lounger and hurries off to the locker room.

Doctors and nurses gulp the bitter lounge coffee, their gentle morning murmuring a continuous low-key hum. Carol and Dr. Severson acknowledge each other with a nod. He's the surgeon on her first scrub. She likes starting out with Severson. All business, no surprises.

Dr. Mason and his two associates are in soft argument this morning. Carol sees Dr. Mason turning his head, seeking her out. For no reason she flutters her fingers in his direction and sees him flood scarlet. His partners' heads snap in her direction, their smiles broad and friendly. They will be working a burn reconstruction. Each man on a different area. Mason has completed eyelids, nose, and right ear, in previous weeks. It's said he worked a miracle.

Carol would have dated Mason if Jeff hadn't been in her life. Her sister introduced them. Handsome, intense in his courtship, Jeff caught her off balance, though the constant sting of caution never left her.

"Grab him," her sister said. "He's crazy about you. Don't you want a normal life?"

Of course she did and when Jeff had the opportunity to go in on a franchise he claimed would secure their future, she gave him her savings. The moment she put the cash in his hands, she knew he would disappear.

The morning goes quickly. On a break, Carol joins Dee Dee and Sadie in the lounge. Carol and Sadie have coffee. Dee Dee is putting on mascara. "I know you think I'm nuts," she says, "but eyes are all they see of us. Mine look so small without make up."

"Who even looks?" Sadie laughs. "Oh, I get it. You're scrubbing with plastics. Dr. Barkley."

Dee Dee rolls her eyes. Snaps shut her mascara case. "He is so cute."

Everyone speaks of Sadie as 'Career Scrub' because, at sixty, she has no other prospects. Five years ago she thought her seniority would automatically qualify her for the head nurse vacancy, but administration brought in Bigelow, an outsider with degree qualifications. Sadie was told she was too valuable as scrub and received a minimal raise. The nursing staff hasn't accepted Bigelow and, except for making assignments, Sadie still runs the show. She's tiny, requiring she stand on a platform during surgery. Sadie wears her scrub cap down to her eyebrows and fairly lunges at affiliating students who want to display a bit of hair.

Informed concerning the surgical staff's personal and professional lives, Sadie discusses them with all the familiarity of an old aunt. They are her family, and her propensity for remembering details can be unnerving. This morning, as Dr. Wexler closed an abdomen and humorously complained of his sister's extended visit, Sadie asked, "Is she the one who made you ride bareback as a kid?" Jolted, Wexler wondered what other gems Sadie had tucked away.

"I heard Dr. Herby doesn't want residents scrubbing with him because he's hung over," Dee Dee says.

"He looks O.K. to me," Carol says.

"Yeah, well Janet's keeping anecdotal notes on him and she says she has a list as long as your arm."

"A man who's lost a son to suicide and a wife to another man might be expected to drink a little," Sadie says. Shaking her head she sips her coffee and sets down the cup. "I don't know about you, but I can't drink this slop. I'd like to know the last time anyone cleaned the coffee pot."

O.R. staff drift in as they finish. Mason pours coffee to be near Carol.

Dee Dee sips her coffee and makes a face. "At least it wakes you up. Carol, you headed for the circus this afternoon?"

Carol nods, "I was, but Bigelow changed my schedule."

Though Sadie can never hope for Bigelow's position, she chips away at the head nurse at every opportunity. "That inconsiderate poop," she storms. "You've been planning your afternoon circus date for weeks. Bigelow knows. Everyone knows it's your yearly thing. Good luck trying to get tickets for tonight."

Interested or not, the afternoon staff are recipients of Sadie's rampage against Bigelow, and Carol's aborted plans.

This evening Mason mills around the circus grounds, watching for Carol. He promises himself a program of recovery if she does not come alone. Tonight he will know, and he steps across trampled grass to the ticket office. 'SOLD OUT' hangs on a chain over the window, but there she is sitting on the edge of the fountain. There's that quick smile of recognition as she lifts her head and shakes short brown hair from her eyes. "Come," he says, taking her hand. "I want to show you something."

They walk around back to the animal barns and wait. Later he will tell her how his father, who could afford so little, always took him to the circus. He will draw her out. He holds her hand lightly. Neither speak. They feel the earth move with the muffled thud of giant feet. Out of the dusk file fifteen silent elephants, tail to trunk. They loom up gray, their trainers mere shadows. He hears the gasp of her breath and they back against the wall, their hands holding tight, as they watch the steady march of the elephants.

Cheney Duesler is a short story writer, novelist and playwright, whose stories have appeared in magazines, and whose plays have been presented in radio and stage readings. She has won many prizes for her work, which draws on settings from her childhood in Michigan's Upper Peninsula, from her work as a visiting nurse in New York City and as a nursing instructor in Wisconsin. Following retirement, Duesler led an active, productive life in Wisconsin before moving to Connecticut, where she now lives.